THE MERIDIAN PARIS PROTOCOL

Things Are Not What They Remember

Mark Anderson, PhD

Become the Story. Become the Storyteller.

Copyright Page

Images are crafted using AI tools constructed by the author.

Mark Anderson, PhD
18 Dover Street Suite 492
Norwell, Massachusetts 02061

First edition
Printed in the United States

ISBN 979-8-9949357-9-8 (ebook)
ISBN 979-8-9958085-0-3 (paperback)

Disclaimer

This is a work of fiction. Names, characters, places, and incidents are either the product of the author's imagination or used fictitiously. Any resemblance to actual persons, living or dead, or actual events is purely coincidental.

The author and publisher expressly disclaim any responsibility or liability for any loss, injury, adverse effects, or damages—direct or indirect—that may result from the use or application of any information, suggestions, or ideas presented in this book. Readers assume full responsibility for how they choose to use the information contained herein.

All product names, trademarks, and registered trademarks mentioned in this book are the property of their respective owners and are used for identification and educational purposes only. No endorsement is implied. Any products mentioned are used solely as illustrative examples as nominative fair use.

Acknowledgements

Thank you to my sister who listens to my many stories with interest.

No timemachines were harmed in the writing of this book.
Several possible habits and choices were examined.

This book exists because of curiosity, good conversations, judgment, purpose, and the quiet patience of people who allowed imagination to evolve.

Dedication

This book is dedicated to everyone who has ever tried to understand story telling and how you choose to tell it.

To everyone who has ever wondered
what it means to live alongside possible futures.

For those who still pause
before accepting an answer.

Contents

Preface: The Conversation Has Already Begun

You are already part of this story.

Not because you chose it.
But because you are already inside a sequence of decisions.

Every path taken.
Every path avoided.

They do not disappear.

They persist—
as possibilities.

Most of the time, those possibilities collapse into a single experience.
A single version of events.
A single life that feels continuous.

But what if they didn't?

What if the system that governs those possibilities
was not fixed—
but adaptive?

And what if someone had to decide
whether that system should ever be allowed to settle?

This book is not simply a story.

It is a sequence.

Each chapter is a moment.
Each moment is a decision point.

Read it as narrative.
Or read it as a model.

Either way—

the conversation has already begun.

How to Read This Book

This novel is structured as a sequence of moments.

Each chapter is not just a scene it is a decision boundary.

You can experience it in different ways:

- **Visually** → Imagine each chapter as a scene unfolding in real time
- **Linearly** → Follow the story from beginning to end
- **Conceptually** → Focus on the system beneath the narrative

The structure is intentional.

Time, decisions, and outcomes matter.

Short chapters reflect transition.
Not brevity.

Pauses matter.
Repetition matters.
Perspective matters.

If you find yourself slowing down— (em dashes and fragments)
pausing—
or rereading a line—

the book is working as intended.

Because the most important moments in this story
are not the ones that move forward.

They are the ones that make you stop.

Dramatis Personae

Elara Voss *(record incomplete)*
Role: The one who remembers; a traveler who resists finality and seeks a system that preserves choice rather than demands it.
Visual Identity: A solitary female traveler with a grounded presence, wearing a long, dark, timeless coat and carrying a weathered briefcase. Her

movements remain natural, though subtly out of alignment with her surroundings.

The One Who Stayed *(designation inferred)*
Role: A version of Elara that did not leave; a fixed point within a closed sequence.
Observed Function: Maintains continuity within a collapsed branch; repeats interaction without progression.
Visual Identity: Indistinguishable from Elara, but motionless in intent, positioned at the edge of the tower against an unchanging horizon.

Elias Vane *(origin uncertain)*
Role: An unexpected presence within the sequence.
Observed Function: Introduces deviation and challenges established patterns of recurrence.
Relationship to Elara: Recognition occurs before understanding; the connection is persistent but undefined.
Visual Identity: A composed, deliberate figure whose presence does not fully align with the surrounding environment.

The Network *(system-level construct)*
Role: An adaptive structure governing continuity across branching timelines.
Observed Function: Preserves, stabilizes, and contains divergent outcomes while permitting controlled recurrence.
State: Partially observable; not fully understood.

The Meridian House *(location / node)*
Role: A convergence point within the Network.
Observed Function: Holds intersections of memory, decision, and sequence alignment; functions as both archive and transition threshold.
Properties: Interior space exceeds external geometry; spatial and temporal boundaries are inconsistent.

The Briefcase *(object of continuity)*
Role: A persistent object carried across iterations.
Observed Function: Acts as an anchor between sequences; contents not fully catalogued.
Condition: Weathered; unaffected by environmental variation.

The Notebook *(fragmentary record)*
Role: A partial record of prior sequences.
Observed Function: Contains observations and patterns that may not correspond to the current iteration.
Limitation: Incomplete; authorship uncertain.

The City (Paris) *(recurring environment)*
Role: Primary environmental constant.
Observed Function: Provides a stable frame for sequence variation despite underlying divergence.
Condition: Visually consistent; structurally unreliable.

The Tower *(convergence point)*
Role: A boundary between observation and decision.
Observed Function: Site of repeated arrival and sequence instability.
Property: Perspective alters interpretation; elevation correlates with awareness.

Prologue: The One Who Stayed

THE MERIDIAN PARIS PROTOCOL

Things Are Not What They Remember

She does not remember when she stopped moving. That is the first thing she notices—not the tower, not the sky, not the city below, but stillness. It has been so long since she has taken a step that the idea of movement feels theoretical. Possible, but no longer natural.

She stands at the edge of the platform, one hand resting lightly on the iron rail, watching the horizon as it repeats.

Sunset again.

It is always sunset here. The same light, the same color, the same suspended moment where the city has not yet decided to become night. She used to measure time. She remembers that. Clocks. Sequences. Intervals. The discipline of forward motion.

Now there is only recurrence.

She closes her eyes. For a moment—just a moment—she almost remembers why she came. A briefcase. A crossing. A decision. Something about not allowing the sequence to close.

Her hand tightens on the railing. Too late.

The memory dissolves before it completes. That is the second thing she has learned. Memory does not disappear all at once. It erodes at the edges—meaning first, then context, then purpose. What remains is familiarity without understanding.

She opens her eyes again. Paris stretches below her, unchanged. Beautiful. Precise. Unmoving in its perfection.

That is the trap.

Perfection is not stability. It is containment. She knows that now…or she knows that she once knew it. The difference matters less each time she tries to recall it.

Behind her, something shifts.

A sound. Not mechanical. Not environmental. Arrival. Her breath catches, just slightly. It still does that. Some reflex remains. She does not turn immediately. She has learned this part too. If she turns too quickly, the sequence destabilizes. If she waits—just long enough—the pattern holds.

Footsteps. Measured. Careful. Familiar. She closes her eyes again.

There it is. Recognition. Not visual. Structural. Someone has reached the tower again. Another version. Another attempt. Another iteration of the same decision.

Her voice, when she speaks, feels distant to her own ears.

"You remembered the market." The words arrive before she fully understands them. But they are correct. They are always correct. That, at least, remains consistent.

She opens her eyes and looks out at the horizon. She does not turn. Not yet. Because she already knows what she will see.

A woman. A coat. A briefcase. Hope. She remembers hope. That is the third thing she notices. It still exists. But not here. Only in the version that has just arrived.

Her fingers tighten slightly on the iron rail.

There was a moment—once—when she stood where that woman now stands. A moment where the choice still existed. She tries to recall it. Tries to reconstruct it. But the sequence is closed here. Locked.

This branch does not move forward. It only continues. Again. And again. And again.

She speaks, quietly now—not to warn, not to guide, but because the pattern requires it. "You still have time to stop." The words hang in the air between them. She knows how this goes. She knows what comes next. She knows this version will not stop. None of them ever do.

And somewhere, deep beneath the erosion of memory and meaning, something in her is relieved.

There was a voice. Not external. Not entirely her own. It did not arrive clearly—only fragments, as if carried through something unstable.

A warning, perhaps. Or a repetition.

You still have time to…

The rest did not follow. Another thought pressed in, quieter—closer:

…before.

She turned, certain for a moment that someone stood behind her. No one did.

Only the feeling remained— that this moment had already begun.

A mysterious briefcase. A notebook. And the quiet certainty that some memories are not your own.

Imagine.

You arrive without warning—no machine, no explanation—
standing alone, a briefcase in your hand.

The city is silent.

No crowds.
No footsteps but your own.
No one noticed your arrival.

And yet… something is wrong.
You are not meant to be here.
And still…you are not alone.

A memory begins to surface—slowly, uncertainly.

You are a time traveler.
But the certainty fractures almost immediately.
Because you feel something else.

You have been here before.

Not in the way memory works.
Not in the way places are learned.

In the way a moment repeats
without permission.

Now… consider the possibilities.
And consider which version of you chose them.

Chapter 1: The Plaza of First Light

Paris was still becoming itself.

At that hour before the city fully remembered its name, the Trocadéro plaza lay in a hush of pale gold and long geometry. The broad stone ground held the cold of night, though morning had already begun to spread across it in bands of amber light. Far ahead, centered in the distance like a thought too large to ignore, the Eiffel Tower rose through soft atmospheric haze.

Elara walked toward it alone.

Her coat moved in slow dark folds around her legs, timeless in its cut and difficult to place in any single decade. In one hand she carried a weathered briefcase, its leather marked by old travel and older weather. Her hair lifted subtly in the morning air. Behind her, before her, on either side of her, the plaza remained mostly empty, as if the city had left this single corridor untouched for her arrival.

She had not intended to come to Paris.

That was the first truth she trusted.

The second was stranger: she knew this place. Not in the ordinary way of maps or memory, but in the way one recognizes a recurring dream by its light. The patterned stones beneath her feet, the measured distance between the balustrades, the exact shape of the tower in that early haze—all of it felt like something she had once passed through while half-asleep in another life.

She slowed but did not stop.

There was a pressure in the briefcase. Not weight exactly. Presence.

She had learned, after too many crossings, never to open it too soon.

The machine inside responded to locations differently. Some places were quiet, some turbulent. Some distorted chronology in small ways—a skipped second, a repeated gesture, a memory arriving before its cause. And then there were rare places, dangerous places, where time did not behave like a river at all but like layered glass. Paris, apparently, was one of them.

The tower sharpened as she approached.

Sunrise slid across the stone in slowly widening planes. Her shadow stretched long behind her, dark and narrow, pointing back toward whatever version of herself had stepped into this city before dawn. She glanced once over her shoulder and saw only empty space and broad light.

Still, unease remained.

She tried to recall the last confirmed sequence: the room in Vienna, the station platform in winter, the watch that had stopped at 4:13 and resumed twelve hours later, the page in her notebook filled with handwriting she did not remember writing. There had been coordinates. A date without a year. And one line, underlined twice:

Go to the tower before the city wakes. Do not trust the first reflection.

She had no memory of writing that sentence.

A distant engine murmured from beyond the plaza. Somewhere below, on lower streets, a cart rolled over stone. A bird crossed the pale sky. The world was ordinary in all the visible ways, and that worried her more than visible strangeness ever could.

She kept walking.

The closer she came, the more the tower ceased to be monument and became structure—iron, mathematics, intention. It looked less like a landmark than a machine built at architectural scale. Not a portal. Not exactly. But perhaps something a portal could recognize.

She stopped at last near the edge of the great open square and faced it directly.

Warm light touched one side of her face. The briefcase hung still at her side.

For a long moment, nothing happened.

Then the latch on the briefcase clicked once.

Not open. Just enough to let her know the device inside had awakened.

She did not move.

The city held its breath with her.

And somewhere in the brightening air between her and the tower, she had the sudden, impossible sensation that she was being watched by someone at close distance.

Chapter 2: The Second Woman

The feeling arrived before the sight of it.

A slight pressure change. A thinning in the air. A tremor so delicate it was less like vibration than hesitation, as if the morning itself had reconsidered continuing. She tightened her grip on the briefcase and stared toward the Eiffel Tower.

Then she saw her.

Not in a mirror. Not in glass. Not even in shadow.

Ahead of her, several paces closer to the tower, a second figure moved across the same patterned stone. The same coat. The same stride. The same briefcase swinging at the same angle. Her outline was semitransparent in the golden haze, and yet impossibly clear. Not a ghost, not an afterimage—a person, offset in time by some unseen fraction, walking where she herself had not yet walked.

The air between them bent faintly, like heat above pavement.

She stopped so abruptly that the leather handle bit into her palm and her fingers firmly gripped the handle in response. She took a long slow deep breath.

The second woman continued.

Light passed through the duplicate figure unevenly. The edges shimmered. Within that body there seemed to be layers, multiple positions not fully reconciled. One shoulder slightly ahead of itself. A hand doubled for an instant, then resolved. Hair moved in two directions at once before settling into one.

The traveler's mouth went dry.

This was not normal bleed-through. She had seen echoes before… temporal residues left in unstable corridors, repeated movements trapped in a location. But echoes did not look back.

This one slowed.

Very slightly, very deliberately, the figure ahead turned her head.

The face was not fully visible, only suggested in profile through glare and haze, but the recognition struck with the force of an impact. It was her face. Not identical in age perhaps. Not even identical in expression. But undeniably hers.

She wanted to call out, yet some deeper instinct held her silent. The realization of the moment caused her to hold her breath. The warning in the notebook returned with sudden clarity.

Do not trust the first reflection.

The duplicate resumed walking.

Long shadows stretched across the plaza. The tower loomed above both of them, one solid figure and one impossible copy moving through the same field of light. The traveler took one step forward, then another. The air thickened. A faint distortion rippled from the duplicate's path, warping the straight lines in the stone beneath her feet.

"Wait," she whispered, though she was not sure which of them she meant.

The figure ahead paused again.

This time, instead of turning, it lifted the briefcase slightly, as though in acknowledgment. Or warning.

Then the haze shifted.

A breeze moved through the plaza. Gold light flared against the iron of the tower. And for one suspended heartbeat the duplicate became more visible than the original—more solid, more defined, more present in the morning than the woman standing in her own body.

Panic rose in her chest, cold and clean.

She quickly dropped to one knee and snapped open the outer clasp of her briefcase, not enough to fully expose the device but enough to touch the emergency switch built into the lining. A small metallic click answered her hand. Stability protocol. Local anchor. Minimal field containment.

The distortion ahead faltered.

The duplicate blurred at the edges, then broke into translucent bands of light that drifted sideways like torn silk in wind. Yet even as it dissolved, the traveler felt—not saw, but felt—the other self watching her with something more complicated than threat.

Recognition. Pity. Urgency.

And then it was gone.

The plaza returned all at once: stone, light, tower, distance, silence.

Her own breathing sounded too loud. She could smell the morning air.

She closed the clasp and stood slowly, scanning the square. No one nearby had reacted. A couple far off near the railing continued walking. A municipal truck moved along a lower road. The ordinary world had not noticed the fracture.

But the fracture had noticed her.

At her feet, where the duplicate had paused, something gleamed on the stone.

She approached carefully.

It was not metal. Not glass. More like a thin, transparent sliver, curved and luminous at the edge like a shaving cut from frozen time. She crouched and reached toward it. Before her fingers could touch it, the sliver dissolved into the air and vanished.

In its place remained only a scent.

Not ozone. Not smoke.

Orange peel.

Fresh bread.

Flowers.

The smell of a market street already awake somewhere deeper in the city.

She straightened and looked away from the tower for the first time.

Paris, it seemed, was not going to reveal itself all at once. It would have to be followed, clue by clue, across its own living surface.

The duplicate had gone.

But it had left her a direction.

Chapter 3: The Hotel Room

The hotel room seemed to belong to no single century.

That, more than its luxury, made her choose it.

It stood behind a discreet façade on a quiet street, the kind of Parisian address people passed without noticing unless they already knew to look. Inside, the lobby smelled faintly of polished wood, old paper, and expensive restraint. No music. No unnecessary brightness. A place designed for people who wanted comfort without attention.

By the time she reached the room, the city had fully awakened. Yet inside, time softened again.

Velvet drapes framed a tall window through which late morning sun poured in pale gold sheets. A lamp glowed warmly near a writing desk. The furniture was dark wood, refined and heavy, with the stillness of objects chosen to outlast fashion. A mirror over the mantel reflected part of the room but not—she noted immediately, the window behind her. That absence unsettled her enough that she turned the mirror slightly toward the wall.

She set the briefcase on the bed and crossed to the window.

From there she could see rooftops, chimneys, terraces, and beyond them the higher line of the city where the tower sometimes emerged between buildings like a fixed point in a dream. She stood with one hand against the cool frame and let the silence collect around her.

Travel across time never felt like motion afterward. It felt like residue. A slight distance from one's own skin. A delay between thought and touch. That sensation was with her now, stronger than usual. The duplicate at the plaza had not merely frightened her. It had destabilized her certainty that she remained the original sequence.

She pressed her thumb into the center of her palm, hard enough to hurt.

Pain, at least, was immediate.

She took out her notebook from the inner pocket of her coat and sat at the writing desk. The pages were crowded with dates, sketches, arrows, fragments of places and cautions written in different moods of handwriting. Some lines she remembered composing. Others looked like messages left by a version of herself who had worked under pressure and assumed explanation could come later.

She turned to the most recent pages.

Paris. Trocadéro. Sunrise.
Look for recurrence near engineered landmarks.
The tower may be an attractor, not a destination.

On the opposite page, written in a sharper hand:

If you see yourself, the sequence has already split. Continue anyway.

She stared for a timeless moment at that sentence.

Outside, somewhere below, a siren passed and faded. Someone laughed in the street. Glass clinked softly from another room or another floor. Ordinary life continued with offensive calm.

At last she opened the briefcase fully.

Inside, nested in dark fabric, lay the device.

It was compact enough to be carried, intricate enough to resist instant understanding. Interlocking metallic arcs surrounded a central chamber in which a pale core light pulsed slowly, almost like breathing. Delicate etched lines crossed its surface, some mechanical, some resembling notation from physics, some disturbingly close to script. When inactive, it seemed like an artifact recovered from an impossible laboratory. When active, it seemed to listen.

The light at its center brightened as her hand hovered above it.

She did not touch it yet.

Instead she looked back to the window and watched the sunlight fill the room. Golden illumination spread across velvet, brass, wood grain, the edge of the bed, the leather of her briefcase. Everything in the room felt quiet, reflective, detached from the ordinary rush of hours.

She realized, suddenly, how tired she was.

Not physically. Temporally.

As though she had been arriving for years without ever fully arriving.

When she finally placed her fingertips on the device, it answered with a faint tone that seemed to resonate more in the bones than in the ear. A ring of symbols lit around the core. One sequence repeated itself three times.

Coordinates? No.

Street names.

Not in words, but she understood them with the irrational certainty the machine often produced.

Market. River. Bridge. Tower.

A path.

She closed the case at once.

The room had given her what it was meant to give: a pause, a frame, a place in which the scattered pieces could briefly stand still. But stillness was not the same as safety. Whatever had split at the plaza was continuing somewhere beyond the window.

And in Paris, the city itself seemed prepared to help it happen.

She rose, took the briefcase, and turned once more toward the sunlit glass.

For an instant, in the reflection, she thought she saw someone standing beside her.

When she looked directly, the room was empty.

Chapter 4: The Market

The market announced itself before she reached it.

Not with sound first, though there was plenty of that... the murmur of bargaining, the scrape of crates, footsteps on damp stone, cloth awnings shifting overhead... but with scent. Citrus. Bread. Wet leaves. Roses. Soap. Coffee. The mingling of fragrances moved down the street like memory itself, layered and impossible to separate.

When she turned into the market lane, the city changed scale.

Paris became immediate there. Hand-to-hand, basket-to-basket, stall-to-stall. Pyramids of oranges glowed in the early light. Bunches of herbs darkened the air with green sharpness. Bread lay in long warm rows, crusts catching the lamplight. Flowers overflowed metal buckets in reds, creams, violets, and pale pinks. Above it all, small lamps still burned against the tail end of morning, their golden halos soft against the waking day.

She walked through it in deliberate silence.

Soft crowd blur surrounded her. Men unloading produce. A woman rearranging tulips. A child reaching for a pastry. A delivery cyclist threading through with impossible confidence. Faces passed without fixing on hers. She remained in sharp private focus inside the flow, coat dark against the warmth of fruit and stone, briefcase heavy at her side.

This, she thought, was what the duplicate had left for her: not a message in words, but a trail in atmosphere.

At the first stall she stopped only to look.

The vendor, a gray-haired man with practiced eyes, held up an orange. "Madame?"

She shook her head. Then, after a pause, asked, "Have you been here long today?"

He shrugged. "Since before the sun. Everyone wants beauty early."

She almost smiled. "Did you see a woman pass this way? Dark coat. Briefcase."

He glanced at her coat, then at the case in her hand, and his expression flickered with uncertain amusement.

"Many women pass," he said. "Some twice."

Her breath caught.

But the vendor was already turning to another customer, perhaps not knowing what he had said, perhaps knowing perfectly well. She moved on.

The cobblestones were uneven, polished by generations of wheels and weather. Light collected in their shallow dips. The air held warmth at shoulder height and chill close to the ground. She noticed small things with unnatural clarity: the fuzz on a peach, condensation on a vase, flour dust on black sleeves, the creak of rope under a hanging awning. Temporal instability often heightened perception before it disrupted sequence. The world became more itself just before it fractured.

At a flower stall she saw it.

Not the duplicate. Evidence.

One white rose among a cluster of pale blooms had browned at the edges—not from age but from time acceleration. A ring of petals was crisp and nearly dust while the stem remained fresh. She leaned closer. Around it, the air shimmered faintly.

"Don't touch that one," the florist said quickly.

"Why?"

The woman hesitated. "Because I put it there only moments ago. And yet it looks like it missed its proper hour."

The traveler straightened.

"Has anything else happened?"

The florist gave her a long searching look. "You are asking like someone who has already seen something." "Have we met before?"

The answer sat between them without being spoken.

At the edge of the stall, beneath a bucket of lilies, lay a thin trail of luminous residue like the fading trace of rain in sunlight. It bent toward a narrower side street.

The traveler followed it.

The market thinned behind her but never entirely disappeared. Its scents clung to her as she walked... orange peel, bread crust, wet stems, lamp heat. The city around her felt immersive, sensory, reflective, as if Paris were not merely a setting but an instrument tuned to resonance. Somewhere nearby, just out of sight, another version of herself had passed through this same corridor.

At the end of the narrow lane she stopped.

The residue ended at a doorway shadowed between two shuttered shops.

Nothing stood there.

And yet the latch on her briefcase clicked again.

This time she opened it a fraction.

Inside, the device pulsed with stronger light than before. It was no longer simply reading the city. It was responding.

She closed the case and looked back toward the market, where lamps still glowed and voices lifted and the whole bright human world went on exchanging ordinary things.

Scent. Memory. Discovery.

Paris was leading her by the senses because logic alone would have sent her away.

The narrow lane smelled suddenly of metal and heat.

It was time to stop following traces.

It was time to open the case.

Chapter 5: The Device

The lane was empty except for light.

Not sunlight alone, though enough of that filtered between the buildings to gild the stone and sharpen the edges of doorframes. This light was concentrated, inward, waiting. It seemed to gather around the briefcase even before she knelt to open it.

She set the case on the cobblestones. Then took a calm breath.

The leather creaked softly under her hands. For a moment she did nothing, listening to the market at her back: a burst of laughter, wheels rattling over stone, the low call of a vendor, a knife against a wooden board. Real life.

Grounding noise. The sort of sound one could hold onto if the world began to slip.

Then she opened the case.

The glow rose at once.

It illuminated her hands, the dark cloth lining, the sleeves of her coat, and the lower walls of the narrow street. The device inside seemed brighter than it should have been in daylight, as though its light belonged to a different register entirely. At its center burned a white-gold core. Around it, metallic arcs rotated by fractions, adjusting themselves to some unseen geometry. Fine channels of light ran through engraved pathways along its surface.

She had built parts of it.

That was the terrible truth.

Not all of it. Never all of it. The device had come to her incomplete, inherited through versions of herself and versions of others. But some of the modifications, the stabilizers, the sequence locks, the emergency dampers... those were hers. Somewhere along the line she had become not merely its user but one of its authors.

The core brightened.

A set of symbols appeared in the air above it, projected not as hologram but as distortion. She recognized one marker immediately: local temporal overlap. Then another: recurrence probability. Then a third that she hated seeing—identity ambiguity.

"No," she whispered.

The machine did not care.

It pulsed again, and a narrow beam of light ran over the cobblestones like liquid geometry. The stones ahead of her shimmered. For an instant the lane contained three different mornings layered atop one another: this one with its quiet sun, another wetter and darker, another crowded and shadowless. They snapped back into one.

She closed her eyes.

"Tell me where," she said.

The device answered in the only way it could. It projected an image sequence into the air: a table by water, a bridge lit by lamps, iron structure overhead, stairs rising, sky burning orange above the city.

The same path, now clearer.

The machine was not offering choice. It was confirming inevitability.

She looked down at her hands in the glow. They were steady, but not because she felt calm. They were steady because fear had crossed into familiarity. There was almost comfort in the machine's terrible clarity. Technology, however strange, at least obeyed patterns. People lied. Memory lied. Reflection lied. But systems revealed themselves through response.

She touched the outer ring and adjusted the containment threshold.

The core dimmed slightly, enough to stop spilling uncontrolled light onto the street. Her breath eased. The nearby walls returned to ordinary shadow. Somewhere at the mouth of the lane a passerby moved by without glancing in.

Good.

Paris might be unstable, but it had so far been discreet.

She studied the device more carefully. Along one lower segment, where the metal met an inset strip of dark alloy, there were new scratches she did not remember. Not damage—writing. Tiny marks cut by hand with something sharp.

She lifted the machine toward the light.

Three words.

Not the first.

Her stomach tightened.

The duplicate again. Or something after it. Some future or alternate self had already handled this device after the split and left her a warning in metal.

Not the first what?

Not the first version?
Not the first path?
Not the first choice?

A pulse from the core interrupted the thought. The projected images repeated: river, bridge, tower, ascent, sunset.

Sequence pressure was rising. Delay would worsen the overlap.

She settled the device back into the case, but before closing it, she let herself look at it one moment longer. It was intricate, technological, quietly intense. Not theatrical. Not magical in any sentimental sense. It had the grounded realism of an engineered object that happened to trespass across the categories by which normal life protected itself.

Then she shut the case and stood.

At the far end of the lane, beyond the market roofs, the sky had begun to deepen toward afternoon.

The path led to the river Seine.

And whatever had written—
"***Not the first***"—
was waiting farther ahead.

Chapter 6: Dinner by the Seine

By the time she reached the river, Paris had softened.

Day was giving way to dusk in slow deliberate color. The Seine carried the light in broken ribbons, gold and amber sliding over dark water. Along one quieter embankment an elegant outdoor table had been set near the railing, its white cloth touched by wind, its candle newly lit despite the remaining glow in the sky. Glassware caught the last brightness. Beyond the river, framed by bridges and rooftops, the Eiffel Tower stood with an almost unbearable composure.

She stopped beside the table and looked at it as if it might disappear.

There was only one place setting.

A meal waited there—simple, refined, untouched. Bread, a plate still warm from a kitchen not far away, a half-filled glass of wine reflecting the sky. No note. No card. No visible sign of invitation except the impossible fact that it was clearly meant for her.

The briefcase in her hand was suddenly heavier than it had been all day.

She set it beside the chair but did not sit yet.

The river smelled of stone, water, cooling metal, and distant kitchens. Soft traffic murmured across the bridges. Somewhere a couple laughed. A boat passed low in the water, trailing a thread of muted conversation and engine hum. The whole scene might have belonged to any ordinary evening in Paris, except for the precision with which it matched the sequence projected by the device.

Someone had arranged this.

Or some version of her had.

At last she pulled out the chair and sat.

The candle flame bent in the wind and righted itself again. The city across the water seemed temporarily suspended between day and night, its windows not yet fully bright, its facades holding the last of sunset. She broke off a piece of bread and realized she was hungrier than she had allowed herself to notice.

The first bite felt almost painful in its normalcy.

For several minutes she did nothing but eat slowly and watch the river. The simple act of taking nourishment while the tower glowed in the distance steadied her more than logic had managed all day. She had crossed years, identities, and unstable landmarks, but here was proof that the body still required the same old things: warmth, food, breath, a chair, a horizon.

Intimate. Solitary. Contemplative.

The mood of the evening did not calm her so much as open a space in which fear could be observed instead of obeyed.

She reached into her coat pocket for the notebook. Between two pages she found something she had not placed there.

A restaurant receipt.

No date. No name. Only a handwritten line across the back:

Eat before the bridge. You'll need to remember your own hands.

She read it twice.

Then she held out both hands before the candlelight.

They looked like her hands. Fine scars at the knuckles. Small ink stain near the thumb. A pale burn mark from years ago. Familiar. Yet after seeing the duplicate at the plaza and the message on the device, even her own skin felt like evidence under review.

She lowered them slowly.

Across the river the first tower lights began to appear.

Beautiful, distant, and fatal in their composure.

Something moved in the reflection of her wineglass. She turned it slightly. For a heartbeat she saw not the table and river behind her, but a different angle: the same table, same candle, same place setting... except occupied. A woman in the same dark coat sat across from her, watching silently. Then the surface trembled and showed only the river again.

She did not gasp. She was past gasping.

Instead she lifted the glass and drank.

"Not the first," she murmured.

The phrase no longer felt abstract. She was beginning to understand. This path had been attempted before, perhaps more than once. The arranged meal, the notes, the warnings... all of it suggested a chain of selves leaving provisions for one another across unstable sequence. She was not improvising. She was inheriting.

The realization should have frightened her more.

Instead it gave her a strange, reluctant comfort.

Whatever waited ahead on the bridge and in the tower, she would not be the first to face it. Others—other hers—had carried this same briefcase into the same evening light and chosen to continue.

She stood, leaving the glass half-finished.

The candle flame fluttered violently once, though the air had gone still.

On the river below, reflected light shivered in a line pointing toward one of the historic bridges downstream.

She closed the notebook, took the briefcase, and stepped away from the table.

The pause was over.

Night was coming.

Chapter 7: The Bridge

The bridge rose from the evening like a sentence half-remembered.

It was ornate without being delicate, built in an age when utility still allowed itself to wear sculpture. Decorative lamp posts lined its length, each already glowing warm against the deepening blue of early night. Underfoot, the pavement held a sheen from old moisture, enough to catch reflections from the lamps and the river below. On the water, the city broke itself into trembling lines of gold.

She stepped onto the bridge and felt at once that she had entered transition.

Bridges were always dangerous in unstable sequences. Not because they connected places, but because they suspended a traveler between them.

Over water, above motion, inside architecture meant for crossing rather than staying, time liked to loosen.

She kept to the center.

The Eiffel Tower was visible in the distance now, no longer softened by dawn or haze but darkening into shape against the bruised sky. Each step toward it felt both chosen and inevitable. Her briefcase swung lightly at her side. Lamps glowed one after another as she passed them, their reflections trembling across the pavement and railing.

People moved around her, but only in fragments. A couple pausing at the parapet. A runner crossing quickly. Two tourists comparing photos. Their voices seemed to reach her from a slight delay, as though sound itself had to decide which version of the bridge to use.

Then the delays began.

At first it was subtle. Her footfall sounded twice. Her shadow lagged by half a step. One lamp appeared to dim and brighten out of sequence with the others. She stopped. So did the city, for a beat too brief for anyone else to notice.

When she resumed walking, she saw another figure halfway down the bridge.

A woman in a dark coat.

Of course.

This time the duplicate was not translucent. Not fully. She was real enough to cast a partial shadow under the lamps, unreal enough for the railing behind her to shimmer through one shoulder. She stood still, facing not the tower but the river below.

The traveler did not approach immediately.

The duplicate lifted one hand and traced a line in the air above the water, as though following a current no one else could see. Then, without turning, she said, "You waited too long in the room."

The voice was hers. Older in tone, perhaps. More tired.

The traveler's throat tightened. "Which one are you?"

"A bad question."

The duplicate turned at last.

Her face was clearer now. Same features. Same mouth. Same eyes, though shadowed by a knowledge the traveler had not yet earned. Rain had darkened the duplicate's coat as if she belonged to another evening entirely.

"Are you ahead of me?" the traveler asked.

"Not in the way you want."

The lamps hummed softly overhead. Down on the river a boat passed beneath the bridge and carried a band of moving gold through the darkness.

"What does 'Not the first' mean?" she asked.

The duplicate gave a small, humorless smile. "It means you're still asking singular questions."

The air between them bent.

For a second the bridge multiplied—three railings, three rows of lamps, three versions of the woman facing herself under different skies. One windless, one raining, one lit by sunset rather than evening. Then the scenes collapsed back into one.

"Listen carefully," the duplicate said. "The tower is not the portal. The tower is the instrument. The top is only where the pattern becomes visible."

"Visible to whom?"

"To whichever self remains coherent enough to see it."

That answer settled nowhere useful.

"What happens if I turn back?"

The duplicate looked past her, toward the city behind. "You won't. You think that would produce safety because you still think sequence is linear."

A tremor passed through the pavement. Not an earthquake. More like a skipped frame in the world.

The duplicate stepped closer. The traveler felt the air cool around her.

"Inside the tower," the other said, "you'll be offered recognition. Don't mistake recognition for truth."

"Why help me?"

The question seemed to strike deeper than the others. The duplicate's expression changed, briefly revealing grief so raw that it made her seem more real than anything else on the bridge.

"Because one of us should arrive before forgetting why we came."

Then she reached into her coat pocket and removed a small object: a key of blackened metal, narrow and old-fashioned, though it carried no obvious lock mechanism. She set it on the parapet between them.

The traveler took a step forward.

A car horn sounded from the far bank. Someone laughed behind her. The bridge flickered.

By the time she reached the parapet, the duplicate was gone.

Only the key remained, cool under her fingers.

She picked it up and closed her hand around it. The lamp nearest her brightened sharply, then settled. Water moved below. The city breathed. The tower waited ahead.

Transitional, reflective, quietly dramatic.

She put the key in her pocket and walked on.

Chapter 8: Inside the Tower

The tower changed everything once she entered it.

Outside, it had been symbol, skyline, destination. Inside, it was structure... iron lattice rising and crossing in disciplined complexity, beams intersecting in patterns both engineered and strangely organic. She stood on an elevated platform within that web and looked out over Paris through a geometry of dark metal and warm fading light.

The city stretched below in soft haze.

Roofs, boulevards, rivers, bridges, windows, movement... all of it seemed suddenly smaller, as though entering the tower had altered not only height but scale of thought. Wind moved through the lattice with a low continuous murmur. Sunlight filtered through the iron in angled gold bands. The briefcase in her hand felt less like luggage now and more like an instrument being carried toward its proper chamber.

Anticipatory. Elevated. Cinematic.

She understood at once why the duplicate on the bridge had called the tower an instrument.

It resonated.

Not audibly, not in any conventional sense. But the entire structure held a field, faint and immense, as if every rivet and beam participated in a standing pattern larger than architecture. Her device responded instantly. Even closed, it emitted a steady vibration against the side of her leg.

She moved farther onto the platform.

Tourists remained elsewhere, scattered, laughing, photographing the city. Yet around her there seemed to be a ring of privacy, a subtle displacement that kept passersby from wandering too near. Paris itself, or the machine, or the instability between them, appeared to be drawing a veil around her progress.

She set the briefcase on a metal ledge and opened it.

The device lit with such force that the iron beams nearest her caught pale reflections. Its projected symbols spiraled faster now, no longer isolated markers but interlocking sequences. A map formed in the air—not of streets, but of intervals. Return points. Decision nodes. Convergences. She saw the plaza, the hotel room, the market lane, the riverside table, the bridge. Not as memories but as active coordinates in a system of recurrence.

Then a new marker appeared directly above the core:

ACCESS REQUIRES KEY

She went still.

With careful fingers she reached into her coat pocket and removed the blackened key from the bridge. It looked older here, as though the iron around her had given it context. Its surface bore tiny etchings similar to those on the device, though worn almost smooth by prior use.

So others had reached this point.

Not the first.

She inserted the key into a narrow seam along the device's side where moments earlier no keyhole had been visible. It fit perfectly.

The core flared.

For an instant the city beyond the lattice beams doubled. Two Parises overlapped: one in warm late light, one beneath storm-dark skies. In one version the Seine reflected gold; in the other it reflected lightning. Pedestrians on the lower platform blurred into alternate positions. A child became an old man and back again within a heartbeat. The iron around her groaned, not from strain but from amplified resonance.

The device unfolded by fractions.

Not mechanically, exactly. More like recognition causing hidden architecture to reveal itself. A central ring rose. Inner arms rotated outward. New channels of light opened. The projected map sharpened into a vertical sequence.

Up.

Of course.

She looked toward the higher stairs.

The tower did not want her here on the platform. This was only the first chamber. A threshold before ascent.

In the reflection on one darkened panel of metal she saw herself... and behind that self, briefly, several others: coat collars different, hair lengths altered, expressions hardened or frightened or determined. They vanished when she turned her head.

Recognition is not truth.

The warning held.

She closed the briefcase again, now with the key still embedded inside the device, and steadied herself against the railing. Below, Paris glowed in deepening evening. Above, the internal stairs rose through iron shadows toward the upper levels where sky would open wider and sequence would narrow.

Whatever the tower was doing, it was focusing.

She took one last look across the city, then turned inward toward the stairs.

She took a long purposeful deep breath.

The climb had begun.

Chapter 9: The Ascent

The stairs narrowed as they rose.

Iron beams crossed around her in increasingly dense patterns, throwing strips of golden evening light and dark shadow across the steps. Each landing opened briefly to air and city before turning inward again. The geometry of the tower became more intimate with height—less like architecture and more like a mechanical interior large enough to swallow a person whole.

She climbed steadily, one hand on the rail, briefcase in the other.

Her breathing deepened. The device inside the case pulsed in quiet rhythm, not with her heartbeat but with something external: the structure, the altitude, the approaching convergence. Every few steps she felt a faint resistance in the air, as though moving upward required passage through thin membranes invisible to the eye.

Determined. Upward-moving. Suspenseful.

The stairs seemed longer than they should have been.

That was the first sign.

The second was the light.

Sunset should have been fading. Instead it lingered, repeating itself in slightly altered intensities each time she rounded a landing. One level glowed amber. The next was nearly red. The next returned to softer gold. She looked down once and saw not the same staircase behind her but three descending sequences overlaying one another, each corresponding to a different hour.

She did not look down again.

At the next landing she found writing scratched into the iron handrail.

Not polished. Not decorative. Urgent.

Keep climbing. The pause is the trap.

She touched the letters with one fingertip. Fresh enough to catch skin. Another self, again, had left it here. The chain of inheritances continued upward.

The tower hummed faintly around her.

A gust of wind cut through the lattice and carried with it the smell of rain though the sky above remained clear. Then came another smell layered beneath it: oranges, bread, flowers. The market. The city was rising with her, or she was passing through preserved strata of it.

Midway up the next flight she heard footsteps above.

She froze.

The steps continued for several beats, descending toward her with measured certainty. Then they stopped just beyond the curve of the stairwell where she could not yet see who approached.

"Are you coherent?" a voice called down.

Her own voice again. Or close enough.

"Mostly," she answered.

A short laugh, dry and exhausted. "That's better than some of us managed."

The figure appeared on the landing above.

This duplicate was the clearest yet. Solid, almost entirely. Coat torn at one cuff. Hair pinned back rather than loose. Face pale with strain. She held no briefcase.

"Where is yours?" the traveler asked before she could stop herself.

The other looked at her with flat intensity. "Opened too early."

That answer carried an entire catastrophe inside it.

The duplicate descended one more step, remaining above her as if unwilling to share a level.

"You're close," she said. "Which means the tower will begin offering you versions that seem merciful."

"Versions of what?"

"Of conclusion."

The traveler tightened her grip on the briefcase. "You keep warning me without explaining."

"Because explanation changes selection." The other glanced upward. "And because some things can only be understood from the height at which they become unavoidable."

The device pulsed hard enough inside the case to vibrate the metal rail.

The duplicate looked down at it with something like hatred.

"Listen carefully. At the top, you may see a woman facing the horizon. Do not assume she is waiting for you."

The traveler stared. "Who is she?"

The other self's expression softened in a way more frightening than severity. "Someone who got there first."

Before another question could form, the stairwell flickered.

The duplicate above her fractured into multiple positions: one collapsing to her knees, one turning away, one reaching toward the traveler as if to pull her upward, one already gone. Then all of them snapped out like lights extinguished at once.

Only empty steps remained.

The traveler stood very still.

The tower was no longer merely unstable. It was crowded.

She resumed climbing.

Upward through iron beams and repeating sunset. Upward through warnings. Upward through versions of herself that had failed, diverged, or perhaps succeeded in forms she could not yet recognize. Her muscles began to ache. Sweat cooled at the back of her neck. The city opened wider through the beams with every level, becoming less a place and more a luminous map of consequences.

At the final interior turn before the top, she found one last message carved into the wall beside the stairs.

Smaller than the others. Harder to read.

Remember why you came before you see who stayed.

She stood with one hand against the iron and closed her eyes.

Why had she come?

Not merely to survive. Not merely to trace anomalies. Not merely to solve the mystery of duplicates and warnings. Beneath all of that there had once been a first purpose. A true purpose. Something about preventing a fracture, or closing one, or reaching a point in sequence before it hardened into permanence.

She opened her eyes.

Above her, the last stretch of stairs rose into orange light.

She climbed toward it.

Chapter 10: Sunset (Pre-Portal)

At the top, Paris became horizon.

She emerged into open air and stopped.

The sky over the city burned in layered oranges and deep golds, the last full light of sunset spreading across rooftops and distant avenues before surrendering to night. From this height the city below seemed to fade softly into atmosphere, its edges blurred by distance and warmth. The wind was colder here. Cleaner. It moved against her coat and lifted loose strands of hair away from her face.

She stood at the top of the Eiffel Tower with the briefcase in hand and looked outward.

For a long moment there was only beauty.

That, too, was part of the trap.

After the compression of stairs and iron and warnings, the openness above felt like release. Quiet. Expansive. Emotional in a way that bypassed reason. The world below no longer looked threatening. It looked complete. The Seine wound through it like polished metal. Bridges linked shadow and light. Buildings held the final fire of day along their edges. It would have been easy, terrifyingly easy, to believe one could simply remain there and let the hour close around them.

Then she saw the woman.

Farther along the platform, near the railing where the horizon opened widest, a solitary figure stood facing west into the glow. The silhouette was unmistakable: long dark coat, still posture, one hand resting on the rail. No briefcase. No visible movement except the slight response of hair and coat to the wind.

Someone who got there first.

The traveler did not call out.

She approached carefully.

The platform beneath her feet was solid, but the air around the other woman seemed less so. Faint distortions radiated outward, bending lines and softening edges. The sunset around her appeared brighter than elsewhere, as though the sky itself had concentrated at that point.

When she was close enough, the standing figure spoke without turning.

"You remembered the market."

It was her voice.

"Yes."

"And the bridge?"

"Yes."

"The room?"

"Yes."

A pause.

"Good," said the woman at the railing. "Then you're still near the correct branch."

The traveler stopped several paces away. "Are you the first?"

At that, the woman laughed softly. Not with humor. With resignation.

"No one is the first anymore."

She turned.

Her face was hers, but older in no measurable way—older in sequence, perhaps, in burden, in accumulated awareness. Sunset filled one side of that face with molten light while the other had already entered shadow.

"What happens now?" the traveler asked.

The woman's gaze dropped briefly to the briefcase. "You open it where the sky and the structure intersect. The tower amplifies. The field resolves. One branch closes."

"One branch?"

"Only one at a time."

Wind moved around them. Below, Paris glowed and dimmed in the slow transition toward evening.

The traveler took another step. "Can this end?"

The woman at the railing looked back toward the horizon. "Everything ends. The real question is whether it ends by collapse or by choice."

The device inside the briefcase gave a rising tone.

No more time for questions.

The older self—or alternate self, or later self, or surviving self—gestured toward a place on the platform where the iron lines of the tower framed a gap of open sky. The geometry there felt exact. Chosen. A junction between engineering and emptiness.

"That is where I stood," she said.

The traveler's chest tightened. "And?"

"And I'm still here."

Recognition is not truth.

The warning returned with absolute force.

She understood then. This woman was not necessarily guide or enemy. She was outcome. One possible consequence standing in visible form, tempting the present toward repetition by the sheer authority of survival.

"Why stay?" the traveler asked.

The woman closed her eyes for a brief second before answering. "Because leaving required remembering more than I could bear."

The honesty of it pierced harder than any threat.

Sunset intensified. The clouds above Paris caught fire at their edges. The city seemed to hold itself motionless beneath the sky. Emotional. Reflective. Anticipatory. Every visual promise of transition sharpened at once.

The briefcase clicked.

She moved to the marked point between iron and horizon and set it down. Her hands trembled now, not from uncertainty but from proximity. The journey had narrowed to this: not merely opening the case, but deciding whether she would accept the offered recognition of the woman behind her or trust the sequence of warnings left by other selves.

She opened the briefcase.

Light flooded upward.

Not harsh. Not explosive. White-gold and impossibly dense, illuminating her face, her coat, the metal around her, the wind itself. The device unfolded fully for the first time, rings rising, inner structures aligning, the key burning dark at its center. Air bent. The city below blurred. The sky ahead seemed to draw inward toward a point not yet visible.

Behind her, the other woman whispered, "You still have time to stop."

The traveler stared into the forming light.

Then she remembered the line scratched into the stairwell wall.

Remember why you came before you see who stayed.

She had not crossed years and fracture and memory to preserve one exhausted branch of herself in eternal sunset. She had come to choose movement over stasis. Closure over recurrence. Truth over recognition.

The air in front of her rippled.

A shape began to form in the light... not yet a door, not yet a wound, but the first outline of a passage.

The city vanished into brilliance at the edges.

Wind tore across the platform. Iron sang. The woman behind her cried out something she could not hear.

And standing at the top of the tower, suspended between the last light of Paris and the first opening of elsewhere, the traveler took one final breath and stepped toward the threshold.

Chapter 11: The Opening

The threshold did not open like a door.

It assembled.

Light folded inward on itself, layer after layer, until the brilliance in front of her became structure rather than glare. The air tightened. The iron framework of the tower rang with a low harmonic tremor that traveled up through the soles of her boots and into her spine. The device within the briefcase shone so fiercely that its metallic arcs disappeared inside their own radiance, leaving only the impression of geometry holding against impossible pressure.

She took one step closer.

The forming passage looked thin at first, as if it were no thicker than glass. Then depth arrived all at once. Not visible depth—felt depth. Distance hidden inside surface. A corridor compressed into a vertical shimmer no wider than her shoulders. Its edges flickered between clean definition and liquid instability. Inside it, colors shifted too quickly to name: silver, amber, blue-white, a bruised violet, then a tone like old film held to the sun.

Behind her, the other woman spoke again, but the words came distorted.

"You don't know... "

The rest vanished under the rising resonance.

The traveler kept her eyes on the opening.

The city below had begun to blur at the margins, Paris dissolving not from destruction but from competing versions. One skyline stood beneath her, then two, then several, each offset by tiny angles of history and weather. In one, rain moved over the river. In another, the sky burned redder. In another, the tower lights had already come on though the sun still hovered at the horizon. The platform beneath her remained solid, but only because the device held it so.

She understood then with sudden terrifying clarity: if she did not move soon, the tower itself would become a chamber of unresolved versions. A place where no branch could decide itself enough to continue.

The woman behind her shouted, "If you go through there, you may not come back as the one who left."

At that, the traveler almost turned.

Almost.

Instead she said, without looking back, "Maybe that was never possible."

The answer surprised her by how true it felt.

She lifted the briefcase.

The device responded instantly. The opening widened by a fraction. Wind surged toward it, carrying with it fragments of Paris: the scent of river stone, hot bread, old iron, oranges, candle smoke, rain that had not yet fallen. The sounds of the city stretched into long thin threads and were drawn into the light.

At the edge of the threshold, her coat began to shimmer.

Not disappear. Translate.

The fabric around her sleeve showed three different textures at once: dry wool, damp wool, ash-frayed cloth. Her hand over the handle of the briefcase doubled briefly, then resolved. Fear came then—not abstract fear, but the blunt animal fear of stepping into something from which no living instinct could guarantee return.

She set her jaw.

And stepped through.

The world did not vanish.

It turned inside out.

There was no sensation of falling. No sensation of flight. Only reordering. Light became direction. Sound became topography. Memory became weather. She moved through a corridor made of overlapping moments, each one pressing against her as though eager to be recognized. A station platform under snow. A room with blue curtains. A child's hand reaching toward a sundial. A laboratory window at night. A field of dead grass beneath transmission towers. A hospital corridor. A bridge she had never crossed. A coastline she had never seen. Faces looked up as she passed, some familiar, some impossible.

Not memories, she realized.

Branches.

The passage accelerated.

The briefcase burned cold in her grip. The device inside it pulsed in powerful measured beats, anchoring sequence by force. Without it she would have diffused into the corridor like breath in winter air. With it, she retained shape—but just barely. The pressure on her body grew immense, not crushing but interpretive, as though the passage were reading her for coherence.

Then, ahead, a darkness appeared.

Not absence. Destination.

She leaned toward it instinctively. The corridor tightened, narrowed, shrieked in frequencies she felt in her teeth. The branching images around her began to spin faster. One sequence caught her eye and held it for a fraction too long: herself standing at the top of the tower, older, still, turned forever toward sunset. Another showed her on the bridge in rain, coat torn, empty-handed. Another sat at the riverside table across from herself. Another lay bleeding in a room with velvet drapes. Another laughed in a city she did not know.

The passage wanted selection.

"No," she said through clenched teeth.

The device flared.

For one brief, merciless instant she understood what the machine was doing. It was not merely transporting her. It was forcing one branch to remain active long enough to choose. Not the safest branch. Not the happiest. The most coherent. The one least willing to surrender itself to passive repetition.

The darkness ahead opened.

Stone.

Air.

Night.

She stumbled forward and struck solid ground with one knee and one hand. The briefcase slammed beside her. The light behind her narrowed violently, collapsing inward with a sound like a thousand pages turned at once.

Silence followed.

Not complete silence. Real silence. Exterior silence. Wind across stone. A distant dripping sound. Somewhere far off, perhaps water. Perhaps machinery.

She stayed where she was, one palm on cold surface, breathing hard.

The passage was gone.

She lifted her head.

This was not Paris.

Chapter 12: The Place Between Clocks

She was in a room with no clear age.

At first she thought it was underground, because the air was cool and the walls rose in shadow beyond the reach of what little light remained. But the space was too tall, too deliberately shaped, too acoustically alive to be merely subterranean. Her breathing returned to her in soft delayed echoes. The stone beneath her hand was smooth in some places, rough in others, as if repeatedly restored across centuries by people who had not entirely agreed what it was for.

She pushed herself upright.

The briefcase lay half-open where it had fallen. Inside, the device had dimmed to a pale exhausted glow. Good. If it had burned brighter in this enclosed place, she might have feared it had not finished with her.

She rose slowly and looked around. Her breathing purposeful and measured.

A circular chamber emerged by degrees as her eyes adjusted. The walls were lined not with decoration but with mechanisms—old, intricate, partly embedded in stone. Rings. Tracks. Counterweights. Pivoting arms. Some bronze, some iron-black, some made of pale metal she could not identify. It looked less like a ruin than an observatory dismantled and rebuilt from different eras of thought. At intervals around the circumference stood tall openings not quite doors, leading into darkness. Above, far overhead, a domed ceiling disappeared into shadow except where faint lines suggested moving components.

Then she heard it.

Ticking.

Not one clock. Many.

Some fast, some slow, some steady, some stuttering. The chamber was full of clocks she could not yet see, each keeping its own private argument with duration.

She straightened and adjusted the collar of her coat.

The phrase came to her without warning, perhaps from memory, perhaps inference.

The place between clocks.

It sounded ridiculous, and yet exactly right.

A narrow shaft of silvery light fell across the floor several meters away. She followed it and found that it came not from a lamp but from an opening high in the wall through which moonlight entered at an angle. Dust moved through the beam like drifting filings.

As she stepped into it, something shifted overhead.

A metallic arm deep in the ceiling rotated with a slow deliberate grind. Then another answered somewhere to her left. The mechanisms in the chamber were waking, responding either to her arrival or to the device she had brought with her.

She crouched beside the briefcase and checked the machine.

The central core still glowed, but weakly. The key remained in place. Around the inner ring, new symbols had appeared—fewer than before, sharper, stripped of decorative ambiguity. One line repeated in stark unadorned characters:

ANCHOR LOCATED

Anchor.

So this place was not random. It was a node. A fixed structure inside whatever greater network of time the tower had amplified. Not a destination perhaps, but a stabilizing chamber. Somewhere branches converged, separated, or were measured.

She snapped the briefcase shut before the device could awaken further and stood again.

That was when she saw the figure across the chamber.

Not a duplicate.

Not herself.

A man stood in one of the dark openings between the wall mechanisms, half in shadow. Tall, still, dressed in a coat too plain to be accidental and too old-fashioned to place easily. He was not surprised to see her. That, more than his silence, made her heart begin to pound.

He stepped forward into the moonlit edge of the chamber.

He was older than she was by perhaps fifteen years, though hard use and poor sleep might have accounted for some of it. His face held the kind of control that had once been discipline and had since become necessity. In his left hand he carried a lantern, unlit. In his right, nothing at all.

"You took the tower route," he said.

His voice was low, worn, and unafraid.

She did not answer at once.

He studied the briefcase, then her face, and gave the smallest nod—as if confirming details in a pattern long expected.

"That means Paris is still functioning," he said. "Barely."

"Who are you?"

He seemed to consider how much truth a stranger fresh from a crossing could bear.

"Someone who arrived before you," he said. "And stayed longer than was wise."

Not the first. Again.

"Where is this?"

He glanced upward toward the unseen clocks.

"A transit anchor. One of the old ones. It has had other names in other centuries, but none of them matter much. The last useful term was Meridian House."

House.

The word did not fit the chamber, and yet perhaps once it had expanded beyond this room, or once this room had been understood differently.

"Am I safe here?" she asked.

He almost smiled.

"Safer than in the tower. Less safe than before you opened the device."

That was fair enough to qualify as honest.

He took another slow step toward her. "Did you see any of yourself on the way through?"

She thought of the corridor, of branches flickering by. "Too many."

"That means the split is wider than I hoped."

He said it like someone tracking weather in a damaged country.

She tightened her hand on the briefcase. "You knew I was coming."

"I knew someone would come. The machine has been trying to deliver a coherent traveler for a long time."

Traveler. Singular. Human enough to be alarming.

"Why?"

The man looked at her then with something like pity, though not condescension.

"Because the network is failing," he said. "And because in one branch after another, you are the one who keeps reaching Paris before the collapse becomes irreversible."

The chamber seemed to shift around her. Not physically. Conceptually. The clocks, the mechanisms, the anchor, the warnings from other selves, the arranged meal by the river Seine… all of it aligned by a fraction.

Not accident. Selection.

She had not merely wandered into a mystery.

She had been one of its recurring attempts at solution.

The man lifted the lantern slightly. "You can ask questions here until sunrise, and you'll still only understand the edges. Or you can come with me now and see the map."

Beyond him, the dark opening led into a corridor where a thin amber light waited somewhere deeper within.

She hesitated only once.

Then she picked up the briefcase and followed him into Meridian House.

Chapter 13: Meridian House

The corridor beyond the chamber was warmer than she expected.

Not warm in the comfortable domestic sense, but inhabited. Used. The air carried the faint mixed scents of oil, paper, metal, dust, and something older beneath it all—stone that had absorbed centuries of human intention and never fully released it. Her footsteps echoed differently here, muted by runners laid over the floor in intervals that suggested both practicality and care.

The man walked ahead with the unlit lantern in his hand as though he had followed this path so often light had become optional. Amber illumination leaked from concealed fixtures set low in the walls. Some looked electric. Others resembled gas lamps refitted by later hands. Meridian House, whatever it had once been, had not been built all at once. It had been added to, repaired, adapted, preserved, abandoned, and reclaimed across generations of minds that each believed they understood only enough to keep going.

That troubled her more than ruins would have.

Ruins implied an ending. This place implied continuity without clarity.

The corridor curved.

On one side, recessed alcoves held shelves stacked with ledgers, brass instruments, rolled charts, and boxes labeled in handwriting from different centuries. On the other side, narrow windows appeared at irregular intervals, though when she glanced through them she saw not exterior darkness but interior shafts, stairwells, suspended gears, and once what looked like another corridor far beyond, crossing at an impossible angle.

"This place shouldn't fit inside that chamber," she said at last.

"It doesn't," the man replied.

She frowned. "That isn't an answer."

"It's the best answer available."

He kept walking.

She would have pressed him further, but the passage opened suddenly into a long room and whatever protest she had prepared vanished.

Tables ran the length of it. Not dining tables, not desks, but worktables... broad, scarred surfaces crowded with maps, instruments, pinned diagrams, glass cylinders, notebooks, lenses, clock faces without casings, and devices in varying states of completion or collapse. Shelves climbed the walls all the way to a mezzanine lined with railings. Above, the ceiling arched in dark timber and iron ribs. Hanging lamps cast steady pools of gold over the central tables while leaving the upper reaches of the room in layered shadow.

It was a workshop, a library, a command room, a sanctuary, and a warning.

Her gaze fixed on the central wall.

A map covered it nearly from floor to ceiling.

Not a geographic map, though pieces of geography had been forced into it. Paris sat at its heart, drawn and redrawn in overlapping transparent layers—different street plans from different eras, different river lines, different building footprints, different phases of reconstruction and war and peace. Radiating from Paris were branching structures made of lines, circles, symbols, dates, and coordinates connecting it to other cities, other sites, other markers she did not recognize. Some lines were bright with recent ink. Others had been crossed out violently. A few ended in burned or blackened patches where the underlying material had been replaced.

The whole wall looked less like cartography than a nervous system.

She stopped walking.

The man finally turned to face her. "This is why I asked if you wanted questions or the map. Most people think questions come first. They rarely survive them."

She ignored the remark.

"Paris is the center?"

"Not the center. One center." He set the lantern down on the nearest table. "A responsive center. An attractor. A city with enough layered history, stable architecture, repeated human traffic, and preserved structural mathematics to serve as a listening point in the network."

She looked back at the wall.

"The network," she said quietly.

He nodded.

She moved closer to the map. Some of the lines connecting outward from Paris were labeled with names she recognized—Prague, Vienna, London, Alexandria, Kyoto, Cusco, New York. Others used symbols only. A few circles around certain cities were marked with notes in different hands: **unstable, burned, silent, lost, flooded, do not route**.

"This is impossible."

"Yes."

"But real."

"Also yes."

She traced the air near one branch without touching it. "What is it?"

The man came to stand beside her, though not too close.

"The simplest wrong answer is that it's a time travel system."

"And the less wrong answer?"

"It's a civilizational continuity network."

She turned to him.

He folded his arms. "The people who first built parts of it didn't think in our categories. Not time travel. Not transportation. Not prophecy. Their problem was survival of knowledge across collapse. Across fire, plague, war, censorship, flood, empire, forgetting. They built structures—architectural, mechanical, mathematical—that could preserve and re-synchronize coherent sequences of memory and action between unstable periods."

She stared at him.

He went on. "Later generations rediscovered fragments and misused them. Some tried to move objects. Some tried to move themselves. Some tried to send warnings. Most of them barely understood the system they were disturbing."

"And you do?" "Understand I mean."

A pause.

"Better than I want to."

That answer landed with the weight of repetition.

Her eyes returned to the map. Paris at the center. Branches reaching outward across centuries and continents. Failed routes. Silent nodes. Burned corrections. Human effort layered over incomprehensible inheritance.

"And what am I?" she asked.

This time the man did not answer immediately. He walked to one of the worktables, opened a notebook to a marked page, and brought it back to her.

On the page was a diagram of branching loops around the Paris node, annotated in several hands. Near the center of the loops, repeated over and over, was one symbol she recognized from the device. Next to it, in recent writing:

MA / recurrent coherent carrier candidate
Shows unusual retention across branch fracture
Keeps reaching Trocadéro before divergence lock

She looked up slowly.

"Carrier?"

He met her gaze without flinching. "You."

Her mouth went dry.

"No," she said. "No. I'm using the device. I'm not... "

"You are using the device," he said. "And the device is using you."

The room seemed suddenly too still.

He continued with a kind of merciless gentleness. "Most travelers fragment too quickly. They forget their own purpose after one or two splits. Or they identify too strongly with the first surviving branch that looks like them and stop moving. You don't. Across multiple branch failures, you retain enough coherence to continue toward the node. Not perfectly. But unusually."

The phrase from the bridge returned to her.

One of us should arrive before forgetting why we came.

She set the notebook down because her hands had begun to shake.

"And Paris keeps choosing me?"

"Yes."

"Why?"

He looked toward the wall-sized map, toward the layered city at its heart.

“Because something in you resonates with a sequence that still hasn’t been closed.”

She closed her eyes, just for a brief moment and thought through recent events. She opened her eyes and took a step forward.

Chapter 14: The Sequence That Would Not Close

He took her to a smaller room lined with clocks.

Not the grand chamber of arrival, nor the long hall of tables and maps, but an interior room designed for concentration rather than awe. Here the clocks were visible. Dozens of them. Wall clocks, carriage clocks, regulator clocks, marine chronometers, stripped pocketwatch movements mounted in frames, pendulums suspended in open housings, escapements ticking under glass. No two kept the same beat. Some were slow and sonorous. Others clicked with insect precision. The combined effect should have been chaos.

Instead it formed a field.

In the center of the room stood a single chair and a metal table bolted to the floor. On the table lay three items: a photograph, a sealed envelope, and a brass instrument shaped like a collapsed compass.

He gestured to the chair. "Sit."

She remained standing. "Am I being interrogated?"

"No. I'm trying to keep the room from choosing the order for us."

She sat.

The chair was colder than the air.

He took the photograph first and slid it across the table.

It showed the Eiffel Tower under construction.

Not a famous staged image. Something stranger and more intimate. The tower rose incomplete against a pale sky. Temporary scaffolding climbed around it. Workers stood on platforms like dark punctuation marks. In the foreground, partly turned away from the camera, stood a woman in a long coat that did not belong to that century.

Even in grayscale, even blurred by age, the shape of that woman struck her like a blow.

"That isn't possible," she said.

"No," he replied. "But it is common."

She kept staring. The posture, the angle of the head, the narrow case in one hand. Not proof. More dangerous than proof. Suggestion.

"Who took this?"

"We don't know. The plate was found in a sealed cabinet in a destroyed node outside Lyon. The image shouldn't exist because the emulsion hadn't been developed yet in the form used there, and the cabinet itself was dated decades later."

He slid the envelope toward her.

She opened it carefully.

Inside was a single folded page. On it, in handwriting that looked disturbingly like her own under stress, were only two lines:

If the first sequence fails, return to the tower before completion. Do not let them anchor the closed branch.

She read it once, then again.

"Before completion?" she said.

"The tower under construction," he said. "One of the earliest major resonant events tied to the Paris node. We think the tower didn't create the attractor. It formalized it. Amplified it. Made a preexisting pattern usable."

The clocks continued their layered argument around them.

She placed the page back inside the envelope and looked up. "Who are 'they'?"

For the first time since she had met him, he seemed uncertain whether to answer.

"That depends on the century," he said.

"That is not good enough."

"No." He drew a slow breath. "There are always people who want continuity. And always people who want control over continuity. At their best, those goals overlap. At their worst, they become indistinguishable until too late."

She leaned back in the chair. "You said I resonate with a sequence that hasn't been closed. What sequence?"

He picked up the brass instrument from the table and set it between them. Its arms unfolded slightly under their own weight, revealing concentric markings and a needle too fine to be decorative.

"Every functioning node in the network maintains what we call open sequences—active unresolved pathways through which information, intervention, or correction can still move. If an open sequence collapses the wrong way, a branch hardens."

"Harden into what?"

"A self-consistent failure."

The phrase hit her with the force of something she had always known but never named.

He continued. "Most branch failures are local. A lost archive. A burned laboratory. A scientist silenced. A disease model delayed. A treaty unsigned. Tragic, but contained. The Paris sequence isn't local."

She watched his face.

"It connects to multiple nodes," he said. "Too many. It sits at a convergence where architectural resonance, political history, preserved urban continuity, and human movement create unusual reach. If the wrong branch anchors there, you don't just lose one line of correction. You lose coordination across entire regions of the network."

The clocks around them seemed louder now.

"Collapse," she said.

"Yes."

Her pulse thudded in her throat. "So all of this—the duplicates, the notes, the arranged path through Paris—this has been an attempt to stop that?"

"Many attempts."

"And all of them failed."

A quiet beat.

"Not all," he said. "Some postponed it."

She looked at the photograph again. The unfinished tower. The woman who might have been her or might have been one more recurring form selected by the network because it matched a necessary pattern.

"How long has this been happening?"

He gave a tired smile without warmth. "How long would make you more comfortable? One lifetime? Three? Since industrial Paris? Since the Enlightenment? Since the first builders marked celestial intervals on stone and tried to store continuity in architecture?"

She had no answer.

The brass instrument on the table gave a tiny click.

Its needle moved.

Both of them looked down.

The needle, impossibly delicate, had shifted toward her.

"What is that?" she asked.

"Sequence indexer."

"And?"

"And it thinks you're closer to the original branch than anyone we've had in many years."

The room tilted—not physically, but morally. Weight settled onto her in a new way. Not heroic weight. Not chosen destiny. Structural necessity. The ugliest and most convincing kind.

She shook her head once. "No. I don't accept that."

"You don't need to accept it," he said. "You only need to decide what to do with it."

The clocks ticked on.

At last she asked the question she had been avoiding since Meridian House first opened before her:

"What happens if I refuse?"

He answered without softness.

"Then someone else tries with less coherence. Or the closed branch anchors. Or Paris goes silent. After that, the other nodes fail one by one in whatever order history finds convenient."

She looked at the envelope, the photograph, the needle still angled toward her.

Then she asked, very quietly, "What did it cost the ones before me?"

This time his silence answered first.

Then he said, "Enough that most of them tried to become outcomes instead of travelers."

The woman at sunset.

The woman on the bridge.

The one at the riverside table.

Not merely duplicates.

Refuges.

Branches that had chosen stasis over the unbearable discipline of continuing.

She closed her eyes.

The clocks kept time without agreement.

When she opened her eyes again, she was afraid of the next question... but asked it anyway.

"And you?" she said. "What did it cost you?"

He looked at her for a long moment, and when he finally answered, his voice was lower than before.

"My name," he said, "was Elias Vane. And I was supposed to be the one Paris selected."

She waited a moment, then said, "I'm Elara."

Chapter 15: Elias

The name settled into the room like a truth that had waited too long to be spoken aloud.

Elias Vane.

He did not say it dramatically. No revelation in posture, no flourish of meaning. Just a fact placed on the table between the clocks, where facts were hardest to sentimentalize. Yet the effect on her was immediate. The room rearranged itself around him. He was no longer simply the man waiting at Meridian House, no longer merely guide or keeper or exhausted witness. He had once stood within the same selection pressure now closing around her.

"You failed," she said.

It was a brutal question disguised as observation.

He accepted it without visible offense. “Not in the first sense. That’s what made the second failure possible.”

He moved away from the table and crossed to a tall clock near the wall. Its pendulum swung in an abnormally wide arc, too slow for its size. He rested one hand lightly against the wooden casing, almost absentmindedly, like someone touching the shoulder of a colleague.

“I reached Paris,” he said. “More than once. I opened the device in the tower. I crossed through. I retained coherence long enough to see the larger structure. I did everything the sequence required right up to the point where it demanded a cost I believed I could postpone.”

The clocks listened.

“What cost?”

He looked back at her. “Commitment.”

“That is not an answer either.”

“It is the only one that matters.”

He came back to the table and stood opposite her.

“You assume the network is asking for bravery. It isn’t. Bravery is temporary. Adrenaline can imitate it. So can grief, anger, guilt, and momentum. The network doesn’t care about any of those. It cares whether a traveler will continue to choose coherence after the narrative reward has disappeared.”

She frowned. “Narrative reward?”

“Discovery, urgency, mystery. the intoxicating sense of being central to something vast.” His mouth twitched with something close to contempt, though it was aimed at himself. “People can survive astonishing things while those feelings are active. Far fewer survive the long work after revelation.”

She understood him more than she wanted to.

“What happened?”

He took a folded page from his coat pocket—not old like the messages she had found elsewhere, but worn by being carried repeatedly. He opened it and laid it on the table.

A map fragment. Not of a city. Of a branching sequence. At its center was a mark beside which someone had written:

EV candidate
high adaptability
unstable retention under loss event

Loss event.

Her gaze rose slowly to his face.

"I had someone," he said. "In one branch, enough of her remained that the sequence could still close if I kept moving. In another, I found a way to hold that branch open longer than I should have. I told myself I was buying time. Preserving options. Refusing false binaries. All the noble language people use when they're really just afraid to surrender one version of love."

He said it evenly, but the steadiness cost him.

"And the network?" she asked.

"I split my coherence maintaining both. Paris stopped selecting me soon after."

The bluntness of the answer hurt more than a confession would have.

He tapped the page once.

"I didn't fail because I was weak in the dramatic sense. I failed because I believed my private exception could remain private inside a system built entirely on connected consequence."

The clocks around them seemed suddenly cruel.

She stared at the map fragment on the table. "Did she live?"

He gave the smallest possible nod. "In one branch. Long enough to teach me exactly how much damage preservation can do when mistaken for fidelity."

The sentence stayed with her.

Not because it was eloquent, but because it had clearly been lived too many times not to become precise.

She stood from the chair and moved away from the table, needing distance from both the clocks and the confession. The room was narrow enough that distance was mostly symbolic, but symbols mattered in places like this. She stopped beneath a shelf crowded with disassembled timepieces and turned back toward him.

"So now what?" she asked. "You hand me the burden you couldn't carry and call that wisdom?"

For the first time, something sharp entered his expression. "No."

"No?"

"No. I tell you what I learned too late and let you decide whether it's instruction or contamination."

He stepped closer, though still leaving space between them.

"The women you saw in Paris—the ones on the bridge, at the river, at sunset—they weren't simply failed versions of you. Some of them were intelligent refuges. Coherent branch structures that learned how to imitate conclusion. The system creates them when a traveler stops moving but still carries enough identity to influence selection."

Her mouth tightened. "You mean traps."

"I mean mercies with teeth."

The phrasing was almost unbearable in its accuracy.

He continued. "A branch that offers rest is not always malicious. That's the mistake. Sometimes it really is trying to spare you. But the network cannot afford to be spared in that way. Closed refuge branches draw coherence out of active sequences until correction becomes impossible."

The woman at sunset. Stillness mistaken for survival. Recognition mistaken for truth.

She understood now why the warnings from other selves had carried such urgency and such grief. Each refuge branch must once have felt like relief.

"And you let one of those form," she said.

"Yes."

"More than one?"

A long pause. The look on his face was not emotional but mixed.

"Yes."

The honesty stripped anger of some of its usefulness.

She looked away. Above the shelves, dozens of tiny reflected clock faces glimmered in glass and brass. Every one of them marking a slightly different claim about time. Every one of them functioning.

"You said Paris was supposed to select you."

"It did," he said. "Then it stopped."

"Can it stop selecting me too?"

"Yes."

"How?"

"By your becoming satisfied with a branch that knows how to resemble meaning."

Her eyes closed briefly.

That had almost happened already. At the top of the tower, in the open emotional beauty of sunset, with one future self standing as witness to surrender. Another step in the wrong direction and she might have mistaken recognizable sorrow for necessary truth.

When she opened her eyes, Elias was watching her with an attention that was neither paternal nor strategic. It was more difficult than that. Respect edged with dread.

"What do you need from me?" she asked.

He did not answer immediately. Instead he went to a cabinet in the wall, unlocked it with a small iron key, and withdrew a flat case of dark wood reinforced with brass corners. He brought it to the table and opened it.

Inside lay a set of thin plates etched with layered diagrams. Transparent, stackable, each marked with routes, symbols, and positional grids. When arranged one atop another, they formed a shifting model of the Paris node and its connected branches. Some lines glowed faintly as if holding residual charge from prior use.

"The map room shows the whole wound," Elias said. "This shows the living edge of it. When you step back and see the full system, you can finally understand the *true extent of the damage.*"

He slid one plate toward her.

At the center was Paris again. Around it, branching loops. One loop in particular pulsed with a faint silver line. It ran from the tower through Meridian House to a cluster of unlabeled markers farther out, then bent back toward the city in a narrow return arc.

"This is the still-open correction path," he said. "Narrower than it should be. More fragile than I like. But alive. Only by mapping everything do we see what's truly wrong."

Her fingertip hovered over the silver line.

"And what's at the far end?"

His expression changed.

Not fear exactly. Recognition of difficulty.

"A chamber below the old observatory line," he said. "A sealed memory vault. One of the earliest Paris relay structures still intact enough to matter."

She looked up. "And?"

"And something there has been trying to close the sequence from the wrong side."

The clocks beat around them.

She drew a slow breath. "So that's next."

"Yes."

"Tonight?"

"If possible."

She glanced at the transparent plates again, at the silver line threading through the wound in the network like a vein still carrying blood to damaged tissue.

Then she looked back at Elias.

"One more question."

He waited.

"If Paris selected me because I resonate with a sequence that won't close… what is that sequence actually tied to?"

His face, which had already held too many withheld answers, became stiller than before.

When he spoke, his voice had changed.

"Someone," he said, "hid a memory in Paris that was never supposed to survive. Not just data. Not a message. A human continuity event. A choice, preserved in living sequence. And every closed branch so far has been an attempt to bury it."

The room seemed to narrow.

"Whose memory?"

Elias held her gaze.

"Yours," he said.

Chapter 16: The Descent Line

They did not leave Meridian House through the way she had entered.

Elias led her past the map room, past the corridor of clocks, past the first chamber where the anchor mechanisms still whispered in uneven intervals. At the far edge of that space, where the wall curved into shadow, he pressed his hand against a section of stone that looked no different from the rest.

It moved.

Not a door in the ordinary sense. A release of pressure. A seam acknowledging alignment. The stone slid inward by a fraction, then aside, revealing a narrow descending passage cut directly into the structure beneath Meridian House.

No light.

No decoration.

Only steps.

"Below the observatory line," Elias said quietly. "Older than the tower. Older than most of the city above it in its current form."

She glanced once back at the chamber behind them.

The clocks continued without agreement.

Then she followed him down.

The air changed immediately.

Cooler. Denser. Less forgiving.

The steps were worn in the center, hollowed slightly by passage over time... yet not enough passage to explain the depth of the wear. That meant something else: repetition. Not crowds, but cycles. The same kinds of travelers moving through the same space across eras.

The walls were close.

At shoulder width, the passage forced attention inward. Her breath sounded louder here. The briefcase at her side seemed to amplify every subtle motion. Somewhere below, far below, something metallic shifted and settled with a distant echo that carried upward through the stone.

"How many have come this way?" she asked.

Elias did not turn. "Enough to leave marks. Not enough to stabilize the route."

That answer told her everything it needed to.

They continued down.

The steps did not follow a simple spiral. They bent at irregular intervals, changing angle in ways that felt deliberate rather than architectural. Once, the passage narrowed so sharply that she had to turn sideways to continue.

Another time, it opened briefly into a small chamber containing a circular stone plate etched with faint radial lines.

Elias stopped there.

"Wait," he said.

She did.

He knelt beside the plate and brushed his hand lightly across its surface. The etched lines brightened for an instant, responding to touch or proximity or something deeper in the sequence. Then they dimmed again.

"Still active," he murmured.

"What is it?"

"Calibration node. It measures coherence."

She frowned. "Of the traveler?"

"Yes."

"And?"

He stood and faced her.

"For now," he said, "you're holding."

Not reassurance.

Assessment.

They moved on.

The deeper they went, the more the passage began to resist.

At first it was subtle... her foot slipping slightly on a step that should have been dry, her hand brushing a wall that felt warm instead of cold, a faint sense that the space behind her did not match the space she had just passed through.

Then it became unmistakable.

At one turn, she glanced back and saw the steps above them split into two descending lines, each leading upward to a different version of the chamber they had left. In one, the light was dimmer. In the other, brighter. In one, she saw a shadow of herself still standing at the top of the stairs, hesitating.

She turned forward quickly.

"Don't look back," Elias said.

"I already did."

"Then don't do it again."

The passage tightened further.

A low hum began... not from any visible source, but from the structure itself. The sound was too low to hear properly, yet too present to ignore. It vibrated in her chest, in her teeth, in the bones of her arms.

The briefcase clicked.

She felt the device inside it responding.

"No," Elias said sharply. "Not yet."

"I didn't open it."

"It's opening itself."

That was worse.

She gripped the handle tighter, willing the latch to remain closed. The device pulsed once, twice, then settled back into contained light.

The hum subsided.

"For now," Elias said.

"For now," she repeated.

The passage ended without warning.

One final turn, one final narrow descent, and then the space opened into something vast.

She stopped at the threshold.

Below them lay a chamber larger than Meridian House, larger even than the upper anchor room. The ceiling rose high into darkness. The walls were not smooth stone but layered surfaces of different materials—blocks, metal reinforcements, structural ribs inserted at different times. The floor spread out in a wide circular plane marked by intersecting lines and concentric rings etched into its surface.

At the center stood a structure.

Not a machine in the modern sense. Not architecture in the conventional sense.

A vault.

It rose from the floor like a cylinder cut from stone and reinforced with bands of dark metal. Its surface was inscribed with patterns that mirrored those on the device, though larger, older, and far more complex. Narrow seams ran vertically along its sides, suggesting it could open—but had not done so in a very long time.

A faint light leaked from those seams.

Not bright.

Persistent.

The hum in the air was stronger here.

"What is this?" she whispered.

Elias stepped beside her.

"The memory vault."

Chapter 17: The Vault That Remembers

They descended the last steps together.

The chamber floor felt different underfoot—less like stone, more like something that had once been molten and then cooled under constraint. The etched lines across it glowed faintly as they crossed them, not lighting the space but acknowledging presence.

The vault loomed ahead.

From this distance, its surface appeared layered with history. Some inscriptions were sharp and recent. Others were worn nearly smooth. In places, the metal bands had been replaced or reinforced, as though earlier attempts to access or contain it had failed.

She slowed as they approached.

The briefcase grew heavier.

Not physically.

Gravitationally.

As though the device inside it recognized the vault and was being drawn toward it by something more fundamental than weight.

"Careful," Elias said.

"I am."

"No," he said. "You're curious."

She stopped.

"That's not the same thing as careful."

She met his gaze.

Then nodded once.

Together, they stepped onto the innermost ring etched into the floor.

The hum intensified.

The seams in the vault brightened slightly.

The device in her briefcase responded instantly. This time, she did not resist. She knelt and opened it.

Light spilled upward.

The vault answered.

The seams along its surface glowed in matching rhythm, as if recognizing a signal long absent. The patterns etched into both machine and structure began to align—not physically, but conceptually, like two systems finally sharing a language.

"What is inside it?" she asked.

Elias did not answer immediately.

When he did, his voice was quieter than before.

"A preserved sequence."

"You said that already."

"This is where I tell you what that actually means."

She waited.

"It's not a recording," he said. "Not a message stored for retrieval. It's an active continuity—held in suspension. A decision, a moment, a branch point that never resolved."

Her pulse quickened.

"A memory."

"Yes."

"Mine."

"Yes."

The word settled into her like a stone dropped into deep water.

She turned back to the vault.

"Why would I hide my own memory?"

Elias stepped closer, stopping just outside the innermost ring.

"Because whatever you knew at that moment was too dangerous to exist in an open sequence."

She frowned. "Dangerous to whom?"

"To anyone trying to control the network."

The implication widened everything.

She looked again at the vault, at its sealed seams, at the light trying to escape without fully breaking through.

"And they've been trying to close it ever since."

"Yes."

"And failing."

"Mostly."

The device pulsed.

The seams in the vault widened by a fraction.

A sound emerged—not mechanical, not quite human. A resonance, like layered voices speaking in perfect synchronization at a frequency just beyond comprehension.

She leaned closer.

The light shifted.

And for the first time, something inside the vault became visible.

Not clearly.

Not fully.

But enough.

A silhouette.

A figure.

Standing within the light.

Her breath stopped.

The shape was hers.

Not a duplicate walking ahead or beside.

Not a branch encountered in passing.

A version of herself suspended in continuity, held in the exact moment before a choice.

She took a step forward.

Elias's hand closed around her arm.

"Wait."

"I have to... "

"If you open it too fast, you collapse the sequence."

She froze.

"What does that mean?"

"It means you don't just retrieve the memory," he said. "You overwrite the branches connected to it."

Her chest tightened.

"How many?"

His grip did not loosen.

"More than we can measure from here."

The vault pulsed again.

The silhouette inside shifted slightly, as if responding to her presence.

Recognition.

Not from her.

From it.

Her voice broke despite her effort to steady it.

"She knows I'm here."

Elias did not deny it.

"Because she is you."

Chapter 18: The Choice That Echoes

The chamber held its breath.

The hum, the light, the faint alignment between device and vault—all of it stabilized into a precarious equilibrium. The kind that could last seconds or collapse instantly depending on what she did next.

She stood at the edge of the innermost ring.

The briefcase lay open at her feet, the device fully active now, its inner structures aligned with the vault's outer inscriptions. The key burned dark at its center, absorbing rather than emitting light.

Inside the vault, the preserved version of herself remained suspended in that impossible moment.

Waiting.

Not passively.

Intentionally.

The realization came with sudden force.

"This wasn't an accident," she said.

Elias watched her carefully. "No."

"She didn't get trapped."

"No."

"She chose to stay here."

"Yes."

The word echoed.

She stepped closer.

Elias did not stop her this time.

The air near the vault felt different—thinner, sharper, charged with a tension that pressed against her skin. The etched lines on the floor beneath her feet glowed brighter now, responding not just to presence but to proximity.

The silhouette inside the vault became clearer.

Her face.

Her posture.

Her expression.

Not fear.

Not confusion.

Resolve.

The preserved version of herself lifted one hand slowly.

Not reaching.

Not warning.

Acknowledging.

The traveler's throat tightened.

"What did you know?" she whispered.

The vault answered.

Not with words.

With memory.

A fragment broke free—not fully released, not fully contained. It struck her like a flash of cold light behind the eyes.

A room.

Not Meridian House.

Not Paris.

A place filled with instruments and people speaking urgently in a language she almost understood.

A diagram on a wall—branches collapsing inward toward a central node.

A voice: **"If we anchor this, the network stabilizes—but only in one configuration."**

Another voice: **"That configuration eliminates corrective pathways."**

A third voice, quieter: **"It becomes permanent."**

Then her own voice.

"Then we don't anchor it."

The memory snapped back.

She staggered.

Elias caught her this time.

"What did you see?" he asked.

Her breathing came fast.

"They were going to close it," she said. "Lock the network into one stable branch."

"Yes."

"And that branch... "

"…removes all alternative corrections."

Her hands trembled.

"It fixes everything," she said. "At a cost."

Elias nodded.

"A cost they were willing to accept."

She looked back at the vault.

At the version of herself who had refused.

"You hid the decision," she said softly.

Not to Elias.

To the figure inside.

"You took the moment before the anchor and removed it from sequence."

The silhouette inside the vault did not move.

But the light around it deepened.

Agreement.

Understanding.

Recognition.

Elias spoke carefully.

"That moment is the pivot. If it's released uncontrolled, the network could collapse into the anchored branch anyway. Or worse—fracture beyond recovery."

She turned toward him.

"And if I leave it here?"

"Then the sequence stays open," he said. "Unresolved. Vulnerable. Repeating."

The words landed exactly where they needed to.

That was what she had been living.

The repetitions.

The duplicates.

The warnings.

All of it the result of a decision removed from time but never completed.

She looked between the vault and the device.

Between the preserved self and the present one.

Between stasis and action.

“What happens if I step inside?” she asked.

Elias did not hesitate.

“You become the moment.”

Her pulse surged.

“And then?”

“You choose.”

The simplicity of the answer was unbearable.

She closed her eyes.

The tower.

The bridge.

The market.

The hotel room.

The descent.

The map.

Elias.

Every step had led here.

Not to discover the memory.

To complete it.

She opened her eyes again.

The preserved version of herself stood waiting.

Not as refuge.

Not as trap.

As unfinished truth.

She stepped forward.

Elias said her name...

but she was already crossing the line.

The light closed around her.

And for the first time since Paris began to fracture...

time did not split.

It held.

Chapter 19: The Moment Reclaimed

The light did not blind her.

It *contained* her.

Not as a barrier, but as a boundary—like stepping into a space where time had been paused mid-breath. The hum of the vault vanished. The chamber disappeared. The weight of the briefcase, the echo of Elias's voice, the geometry of Paris—

—all of it fell away.

And then...

She was standing somewhere else.

A room.

Bright. Clinical. Precise.

Walls lined with instruments she did not recognize but somehow understood. Surfaces alive with data—branching diagrams, cascading probabilities, layered timelines folding in on themselves.

At the center of the room stood a circular platform.

And around it—

people.

Scientists. Engineers. Observers. Some watching the data, some watching *her.*

And at the far edge—

the console.

She knew it immediately.

Not because she remembered it.

Because she had *built* it.

The realization hit with absolute clarity.

This was not just a memory.

This was the origin point.

"You're early," a voice said.

She turned.

A woman stood beside one of the data arrays—mid-40s, sharp presence, eyes that had seen too many models collapse and still kept building new ones.

Dr. Ionescu.

The name surfaced without effort.

"You said you needed more time," Ionescu continued. "We don't have it."

The traveler looked back at the platform.

At the branching model suspended above it.

Thousands of possible timelines.

Collapsing.

Not randomly.

Converging.

"What changed?" she asked.

Ionescu didn't hesitate. "The network is stabilizing itself."

"That's not possible."

"It is if enough nodes synchronize."

A pause.

Then...

"They're forcing alignment."

The words settled like a fracture forming beneath the surface.

The traveler stepped closer to the platform.

The branching model responded instantly—lines shifting, recalculating, compressing toward a single dominant path.

"How many branches are we losing?" she asked.

Ionescu answered quietly.

"All but one."

Chapter 20: The Argument That Defines Time

The room was no longer calm.

It had crossed the threshold into urgency—the kind that lives just beneath panic but still believes it can be avoided.

Voices overlapped.

Systems recalculated.

And the central model continued its slow, inevitable collapse.

One branch rising.

All others fading.

The traveler stood at the console.

Her hands hovered above it.

Not yet touching.

Behind her, another voice spoke.

"You're hesitating."

She turned.

A man she hadn't noticed before stepped forward—older, composed, carrying the weight of decisions already made.

Director Halberg.

"We don't have the luxury of philosophical debate," he said. "The system is stabilizing. We can either guide it or let it finalize itself without oversight."

"And if we guide it?" she asked.

"We ensure consistency."

She held his gaze.

"At the cost of everything else."

Halberg didn't flinch.

"At the cost of uncertainty," he corrected.

The distinction was deliberate.

And dangerous.

Ionescu stepped in.

"You're not just removing uncertainty," she said. "You're removing adaptability."

Halberg shook his head. "We're removing chaos."

"The same thing," Ionescu replied.

The traveler listened.

But she wasn't hearing them anymore.

She was watching the model.

Watching the branches disappear.

Each one a possibility.

A correction.

A future that might be needed.

Gone.

Because stability demanded simplicity.

"What happens after?" she asked quietly.

Halberg answered.

"After what?"

"After it stabilizes."

He gestured to the model.

"We maintain it."

"For how long?"

"As long as necessary."

Her voice sharpened.

"And if it's wrong?"

A silence fell.

Not uncertainty.

Refusal.

"There is no 'wrong,'" Halberg said finally. "There is only the branch that survives."

The words echoed.

Cold.

Absolute.

Final.

The traveler turned back to the console.

The model was almost complete now.

The dominant branch fully formed.

Everything else...

ghosts.

Chapter 21: The Decision That Cannot Be Undone

Her hands lowered onto the console.

Not abruptly. Not with hesitation.
But with the quiet precision of someone who understood that movement itself had consequences now.

The surface responded before her fingers fully settled.

The system recognized intent—not touch.

Access granted.
Control transferred.

A soft shift moved through the room—not sound, not light, but something closer to alignment. The air seemed to settle into place, as if the space itself had been waiting for this moment to resolve its own uncertainty.

The room stilled.

Even Halberg stopped speaking.

Not because he chose to.

Because something in the environment had removed the need for interruption.

Because now...

it was hers.

Three options appeared.

They did not arrive all at once. They formed—quietly, precisely—resolving into clarity the way a reflection settles when the surface beneath it becomes still.

Not labeled.

They didn't need to be.

She understood them immediately.

Not as choices presented...

but as outcomes she had already seen.

Option 1: Allow stabilization
Do nothing.
Let the network collapse into the dominant branch.
Permanent.
Clean.
Controlled.

Option 2: Force stabilization
Intervene.
Shape the final branch.
Ensure it aligns with human intent.
Still permanent.
Still singular.

Option 3: Prevent stabilization
Interrupt the convergence.
Preserve all branches.
Leave the network open.
Unresolved.
Unstable.
Alive.

Her breath slowed.

Not intentionally. It adjusted on its own, syncing with something deeper than thought.

The room faded.

Not physically.

Irrelevantly.

The edges of the space remained—the console, the figures behind her, the distant architecture of the system—but they no longer held weight.

Because this...

this was the only moment that mattered.

Behind her, Halberg spoke again.

"Make the decision."

Not a request.

A command.

The tone cut cleanly through the stillness, but it did not break it. It simply existed within it, sharp and defined.

Ionescu said nothing.

But her silence was not absence.

It was presence without interference.

It was witness.

The traveler closed her eyes.

And for a moment—

just a moment—

she saw everything.

Not as images alone.

As trajectories.

As consequences unfolding beyond the point of choice.

A world where the network stabilized.

Clean.

Predictable.

Fixed.

The movement of time became linear again—efficient, measurable, contained.

And slowly...

wrong.

Not immediately. Not catastrophically.

But subtly, inevitably—

because no system that cannot change can survive what it cannot anticipate.

The future narrowed.

Then hardened.

Then held.

A world where the network was guided.

Better.

Smarter.

Human-shaped.

Decisions refined. Outcomes improved. Variance reduced.

And still—

limited.

Because control, however precise, is still a form of narrowing.

Because intention replaces possibility.

Because even the best version of a single path is still only one path.

And a world—

fractured.

Messy.

Unstable.

Branches expanding, intersecting, diverging again before settling.

Alive with possibility.

Dangerous. Very dangerous.

Correctable.

Real.

Not predictable.

Not safe.

But capable of becoming something no system could define in advance.

She opened her eyes.

The console waited.

Not passively.

Expectantly.

The network held its breath.

Not metaphorically—there was a suspension, a pause in motion so complete it felt like the absence of time itself.

Time—

for the first time—

did not move forward.

It did not press.

It did not resolve.

It waited for her to define it.

"I won't anchor it," she said.

Halberg stepped forward instantly.

The movement broke the stillness—but only for him.

"You don't get to make that call alone."

"I already have."

"You're risking everything."

She turned to face him.

Not quickly.

Deliberately.

As if the act of turning was itself a boundary.

"No," she said.

"I'm preserving it."

There was no force in her voice.

No escalation.

Only certainty.

Her hand moved.

Not to select.

To remove.

The distinction mattered.

She accessed the core sequence.

Not searching—finding.

The exact moment of convergence.

The point where all branches narrowed toward resolution.

And instead of completing it—

she cut it out.

The system reacted violently.

Not as a single failure—but as a cascade.

Alarms fractured the air—overlapping, unsynchronized. Light shifted in sharp, uneven pulses. The structured pathways of the network began to splinter outward again—

branches exploding outward again—

but without anchor.

Without resolution.

Without the quiet force that had been drawing them together.

"Stop!" Halberg shouted.

The word arrived too late.

It did not reach the action.

It only followed it.

But it was already done.

She turned to Ionescu.

The movement was smaller this time.

Quieter.

But no less final.

"Hide it."

Ionescu didn't ask what she meant.

She understood.

Not because it had been explained...

but because there was only one thing left that could be hidden.

"The moment," the traveler said. "This decision. Remove it from the network."

"That will destabilize everything."

"Yes."

"And you?"

The question did not carry accusation.

Only clarity.

The traveler looked at the collapsing system.

At the expanding branches.

At the chaos she had just restored.

Not as destruction.

As release.

"I'll hold it," she said.

Chapter 22: The One Who Stayed

The vault returned.

Not with force. Not with transition.

It revealed itself—gradually, as if it had always been present and only now allowed to be seen again.

But not as it had been.

The geometry held, the light remained, the boundaries were familiar—but something within it had shifted. Not in structure.

In meaning.

Now...

she understood it.

She stood inside the cylinder of light.

The illumination was not harsh. It did not blind or overwhelm. It held her—defined her position without confining it.

Not trapped.

Anchored.

The distinction settled into her without resistance.

The decision suspended around her.

Not visible as an object, not contained in any single point—but present, distributed through the space itself, as if every surface, every line of light, carried some fraction of its weight.

The moment preserved.

Not paused.

Not delayed.

Held.

Not allowed to resolve.

Outside—

time fractured.

Not as destruction.

As repetition.

Moments folding back into themselves. Sequences adjusting mid-motion. Outcomes arriving, then shifting, then arriving again in altered form.

Repeated.

Adapted.

Survived.

The world did not collapse.

It continued.

But not cleanly.

Inside—

she remained.

The stillness here was not absence.

It was containment. It was different.

Holding the line between possibility and permanence.

Not choosing between them—

preventing one from eliminating the other.

And now—

for the first time—

she was not alone.

The awareness came before the sight.

A shift in presence. A change in balance.

Then—

the other version of herself came into focus.

Because the version of herself who had returned—

the one who walked through Paris, through memory, through fracture—

stood before her.

Not approaching.

Not arriving.

Simply there.

As if both had reached this moment from different directions at the exact same time.

Two selves.

One decision.

One moment.

Finally complete.

The preserved version spoke first.

"You came back."

The voice was the same.

Not echoed.

Not altered.

But it carried a different weight—less uncertainty, more continuity, as if it had been speaking from within this moment for longer than time could measure.

The traveler nodded.

"I had to understand."

The words felt different here.

Less like explanation.

More like confirmation.

"And now?"

The question did not press.

It opened.

"You still have time to stop."

"You said that before."

"I always do."

The repetition did not feel redundant.

It felt necessary.

A structure returning to itself, not to trap, but to test whether it would hold.

A pause.

Not hesitation.

Integration.

The space between them did not empty.

It filled—with alignment, with recognition, with the quiet merging of two perspectives that had once been separate.

"Now I choose again," she said.

The light shifted.

Not violently.

Not suddenly.

It adjusted.

The lines that defined the cylinder softened, then sharpened again, as if recalibrating around a new center.

The vault trembled.

Not from instability—

from response.

Because this time—

the decision would not be removed.

It would not be hidden.

It would not be deferred beyond reach.

It would be lived.

Chapter 23: The Second Choice

The vault did not open.

There was no movement in the walls, no separation, no visible transition from one state to another.

It shifted.

Not physically—but structurally, in the way a pattern shifts when a new element enters it and forces everything else to re-evaluate its position.

The light held, but its alignment changed. Lines that had once felt fixed now seemed to reorient around a center that no longer remained constant.

Like a system recognizing a condition it had never been designed to process:

The decision had returned… with awareness.

The space did not reject it.

It adjusted.

The two versions of her stood within the same moment.

No longer separated by time.

No longer preserved and active.

Now...

concurrent.

The word did not need to be spoken.

It was evident in the way neither version dominated the space, neither deferred to the other. They existed in parallel—not as copies, but as states that had arrived at the same point through different paths.

"You removed this once," the preserved version said.

"Yes."

"And now you've brought it back."

"Yes."

The exchange did not feel repetitive.

It felt like something being confirmed from both sides at once.

A pause.

Not empty.

Held.

Then:

"Why?"

The question did not carry challenge.

It carried weight.

The traveler looked beyond her—

past the light,

past the vault,

into something that did not present itself visually, but could still be perceived.

Depth without distance.

Structure without boundary.

"I thought the problem was the choice," she said.

"It wasn't."

The vault responded.

Not with sound.

Not with force.

With organization.

The light around them began to reorganize—not expanding, not collapsing, but mapping.

Lines formed where there had been none. Surfaces that once felt continuous now revealed subtle variations in density, in direction, in possibility.

For the first time—

the full structure of the network became visible.

Not as lines.

Not as branches.

But as a field.

A continuous, shifting topology of probability, correction, deviation, convergence.

It did not sit still long enough to be fully understood.

It moved—constantly, quietly—rebalancing itself in response to something that had changed at its core.

Alive.

"The problem," she said quietly,

"was removing the moment from time."

The words did not echo.

But the space around them seemed to absorb them, as if testing their validity against what it now revealed.

The preserved version of her studied this.

Not analytically.

Recognitively.

Understanding came instantly.

Not because it was explained...

but because it had always been there, waiting to be seen this way.

"If the moment exists…"

"…the system can reference it."

"And adapt."

"And correct."

Behind them, the vault trembled.

This time, the motion was more noticeable—not violent, not unstable, but unfamiliar.

The structure was responding to something it had not previously encountered.

Because this was something new.

Not stability.

Not chaos.

Something else.

Something that did not resolve.

Something that continued.

"Then we don't choose once," the preserved version said.

"We choose continuously."

The statement did not close the question.

It expanded it.

The traveler nodded.

Not in agreement alone—

but in recognition of what that meant.

The choice was no longer a moment.

It was a condition.

Chapter 24: The Living Network

The device rose from the open briefcase.

Not abruptly.

Not with force.

It lifted with a kind of quiet certainty, as if it had been waiting for the moment when it no longer needed to be carried.

For a brief instant, it hovered just above the edge—suspended between containment and release.

It no longer needed her hand.

The absence of contact did not feel like loss.

It felt like completion.

It had become something else—

a mediator.

Not in form.

In function.

Something that did not control, did not enforce—

but connected.

Between fixed reality and living possibility.

Elias stood outside the vault.

The light did not reach him fully. It held at the boundary, as if recognizing a distinction that had not yet been crossed.

For the first time—

he stepped forward with purpose.

Not drawn.

Not compelled.

Chosen.

Into the light.

The transition was subtle, but undeniable. The moment he crossed the threshold, the space acknowledged him—not with change, but with inclusion.

"This wasn't supposed to happen," he said.

The words carried less resistance than before.

More recognition.

"No," she replied.

"It was supposed to end."

The network unfolded around them.

Not as a structure imposed from above.

Not as a system activating.

But as something revealing itself in response to what had been allowed.

Not collapsing.

Not stabilizing.

But breathing.

The movement was continuous—not chaotic, not ordered in any rigid sense—but alive with adjustment. Lines formed and dissolved before they could fully settle. Paths intersected, separated, then rejoined in altered configurations.

Branches forming.

Rejoining.

Correcting.

Not eliminated...

retained.

The space did not erase deviation.

It absorbed it.

Halberg's outcome had been avoided.

The absence of it was clear—not as a missing piece, but as a pressure that no longer shaped the system.

But what replaced it was not disorder.

Not failure.

Something quieter.

More stable in a different way.

"Adaptive continuity," Elias whispered.

The words felt like something discovered, not declared.

The system had found a third state.

Not by design.

By necessity.

The network no longer seeks a single stable branch

The realization did not appear as a statement—it emerged through observation. Paths that once would have narrowed now held their shape longer, allowed to persist without immediate correction.

It no longer allows unbounded divergence

Where expansion began to exceed coherence, the structure responded—not by cutting it away, but by redirecting, softening, bringing it back into relation with the whole.

Instead, it maintains a reference anchor moment (the vault)

The light around them pulsed—not visibly, but in presence—as if the vault itself had become a point of constant comparison.

All branches continuously compare against this moment

The field adjusted in real time—each variation measured not against a fixed rule, but against what had been preserved.

Deviations are not erased—they are weighted, corrected, or reinforced

Some paths strengthened. Others faded. None were simply removed.

The vault becomes:

A Dynamic Temporal Reference Frame

The words did not feel imposed.

They felt like the only way to describe what was already happening.

Not fixed.

Not removed.

Observed. Re-evaluated. Lived.

Elias stepped slightly closer, his gaze tracking the movement—not trying to control it, not trying to fully understand it, but following its behavior as it revealed itself.

"This is impossible," he said.

There was no disbelief in it.

Only recognition of scale.

"No," she replied.

"It just wasn't allowed before."

Chapter 25: The One Who Remains

The system stabilized.

Not into silence.

Into motion.

The shift was subtle at first—almost imperceptible—but it carried through everything at once. The surrounding structure no longer felt like it was trying to resolve itself. It moved instead, continuously, as if stability had been redefined as the ability to adjust rather than the need to settle.

The two versions of her stood facing each other.

Not mirrored.

Not opposing.

Aligned.

There was no distance between them that mattered—only the presence of two paths that had reached the same point from different directions.

Now there was only one question left.

"If the moment stays," the preserved version said,

"someone has to hold it."

The words did not echo.

They settled.

The traveler understood immediately.

Not as a conclusion reached.

As something she had already known, now spoken aloud.

"Not hold it," she said.

"Live it."

The difference mattered.

It shifted the meaning of the choice from containment to participation—from preserving something outside herself to becoming inseparable from it.

"If no one is here," Elias said,

"the reference collapses."

His voice carried through the space without disturbing it, as if it had been accounted for in advance.

"And if someone is?" she asked.

"They become part of the system."

He did not say it as a warning.

He said it as a fact.

Something that had already been tested, already proven.

She looked at her other self.

At the version who had already sacrificed everything once.

There was no visible sign of that sacrifice—no damage, no change in form—but it was present in the stillness, in the way that version did not move toward or away from the moment.

"You don't have to stay," she said.

The words were quiet.

Not an argument.

An offering.

"I already did," the preserved version replied.

The response did not carry resistance.

It carried continuity.

A quiet realization passed between them.

Not spoken.

Not negotiated.

Understood.

"You shouldn't have to do it again."

The light shifted.

Not violently.

Gently.

The edges of the cylinder softened, then reformed, as if the space itself were adjusting to accommodate a decision not yet made.

Like a system offering a choice instead of demanding one.

The traveler closed her eyes and took a refreshing deep breath.

The air felt different now—not heavier, not lighter—but present in a way it hadn't been before, as if every part of the moment had settled into clarity.

And for the first time she felt the full weight of identity.

Not who she had been.

Not who she might become.

But what it meant…

to be the one who decides.

The realization did not overwhelm her.

It steadied her.

When she opened her eyes,

only one of them remained.

There was no transition.

No visible merging.

Just absence where there had once been two—and a presence that now carried both.

Elias didn't move.

But something in his expression changed.

Not dramatically.

Not enough for anyone else to notice.

Recognition.

As if he had been waiting for this exact outcome—not predicting it, but knowing he would recognize it when it happened.

"Which one are you?" he asked.

Elara picked up the briefcase.

The motion was simple.

Familiar.

Grounding.

Closed it.

The latch settled with a quiet finality—not ending anything, but containing it in a new way.

The device settled inside—

but not inactive.

Just… integrated.

Its presence no longer separate from what had happened.

Part of it.

"I'm the one who stayed," she said.

The words carried no emphasis.

No need for it.

"This is only one possibility…
The choice for now."

At first, it seemed like time was breaking.

Later, it became clear—

It had never been stable.

Epilogue: The City That Remembers

Paris was unchanged.

And completely different.

The distinction revealed itself slowly—not in the structures, not in the skyline, but in the way moments unfolded. The city no longer felt like it was repeating patterns beneath the surface. It moved forward now, but not in a straight line.

The market still moved.

Voices layered over one another, vendors calling, footsteps crossing stone worn smooth by centuries.

The bridge still held.

Its weight unchanged, its purpose constant, spanning distance without question.

The tower still rose.

Exact. Familiar. Unavoidable.

But now—

nothing repeated.

Not exactly.

Small differences.

A gesture that ended a fraction earlier than it should have.

A glance that lingered just long enough to change its meaning.

Subtle corrections.

Moments that almost aligned—

but didn't.

And in that space between expectation and variation—

something new lived.

The network was working.

The traveler walked through the city.

Not with urgency.

Not with hesitation.

No longer searching.

No longer chasing echoes.

Her movement carried a quiet awareness—not of what might repeat, but of what might emerge.

Now...

she was part of the system that made them possible.

Stable, for the moment.

At the Trocadéro...

she stopped.

Took a long, slow breath.

The air felt grounded—real in a way that no longer depended on certainty.

And remembered everything.

Not as fragments.

Not as sequences.

But as something continuous.

The Eiffel Tower stood in perfect symmetry ahead.

Golden light stretched across the stone, catching edges and surfaces, defining space without fixing it.

A bright vertical sliver of light appeared before her.

It did not tear the air.

It revealed it.

She blinked her eyes—

For a moment—

just a moment—

the air shimmered.

And there—

ahead of her—

a second figure appeared.

Not identical.

Not past.

Not future.

Just different.

A different traveler.

The presence did not distort the space.

It belonged to it.

She didn't follow.

She didn't call out.

She quietly watched.

Because now...

she understood.

Not everything required intervention.

Not everything required resolution.

The network remained active.

Not visible.

But undeniable.

New anomalies were possible.

Not as errors.

As expressions.

She may be the guardian, the observer, the participant...

but she was no longer the center.

Remaining unknowns moved quietly beneath the surface:

broken nodes that had not yet revealed their consequence,

multiple travelers whose paths had not yet intersected,

different cities,

different times,

different decisions—

all coexisting within the same living system.

The network was never meant to choose a single path.

It was meant to remember how to choose.

There was no perfect timeline.

No fixed outcome waiting to be discovered.

Truth was not a destination.

It was a continuous decision-making process.

Time was not a fixed path—

but an adaptive system.

And still...

questions remained.

Epilogue Reflection

The system did not choose a single path.

It learned how to remain open.

And in doing so—

it became something closer to life.

Optional Note on the System (For Technical Readers)

The temporal system described in this book can be interpreted as:

- A **dynamic network of branching states**
- A **non-linear decision architecture**
- A **self-correcting adaptive system**

Key concepts include:

- Branch preservation vs. branch elimination
- Anchor points as reference states
- Continuous decision loops instead of fixed outcomes

This is not simply physics.
But it is inspired by systems thinking, AI alignment, and
complex adaptive models.

About the Author

Mark Anderson, PhD

Mark Anderson writes at the intersection of artificial intelligence, human decision-making, and complex systems.

With over 25 years of experience in scientific, regulatory, and technical domains, his work focuses on how intelligent systems interact with human judgment—especially in environments where precision, risk, and uncertainty must coexist.

His writing blends:

- Scientific realism
- Philosophical exploration
- Narrative-driven learning

He is also the creator of the *"With Purpose"* language learning series and multiple AI-focused publications.

The origin of Elara comes from Greek mythology. She was a mortal woman loved by Zeus. To protect her from Hera, Zeus hid her beneath the Earth. In mythology, she became the mother of Tityos, a giant.

Style Notes

This book is written a little differently—on purpose.

You may notice short lines.
Intentional pauses.
Moments that feel incomplete or unresolved.

Some thoughts trail off… suggesting uncertainty or hesitation.
Some break apart—shifting meaning mid-sentence.
Others move more fluidly, carrying ideas forward with a quieter rhythm.

At times, punctuation is used more expressively than traditionally:
— dashes to shift or interrupt a thought
… ellipses to suggest hesitation or uncertainty
, commas to soften the flow of a sentence

White space is part of the experience.
It allows room for reflection—for the moment between understanding and choice.

These are not formatting mistakes.
They are part of how the story is meant to be read.

Some scenes are meant to land quickly.
Others are meant to linger.

If you find yourself slowing down, rereading a sentence, or pausing between paragraphs,
the book is working exactly as intended.

That quiet moment of awareness—the instant you step back and observe your own thinking—
is where the most important conversations in this story truly begin.

This is a story meant to be experienced as much as it is read.

"The structure uses intentional pacing, fragmentation, and punctuation to reflect uncertainty, decision-making, and perception in time."

Author's Intent

This story explores a simple question with complex consequences:

What if time is not meant to be solved—but continuously understood?

We often search for optimal outcomes, stable answers, and permanent solutions.
But systems—biological, technological, and human—rarely thrive under permanence alone.

This novel examines:

- The tension between stability and adaptability
- The cost of eliminating uncertainty
- The role of human judgment within intelligent systems
- The idea that truth may not be fixed—but maintained

At its core, this is not a story only about time travel.

It is a story about **decision-making under uncertainty**.

And what it means to live with those decisions.

Description

THE MERIDIAN PARIS PROTOCOL

Things Are Not What They Remember

What if time was never meant to be fixed?

A solitary traveler arrives in Paris. At first, the city feels familiar—quiet streets, warm light, and the steady rhythm of life unfolding. But something begins to shift. Moments repeat. Reflections move before she does. And just ahead, always out of reach, another version of herself appears.

Drawn into a hidden network beneath the city, she uncovers a system designed to do the impossible: stabilize time itself. But stability comes at a cost. One path. One outcome. No correction. No second chances.

As the system begins to collapse toward a single irreversible future, she is forced to confront a final decision: fix time forever, or keep it alive—and uncertain.

The Meridian Paris Protocol blends atmospheric storytelling with scientific and philosophical depth, exploring the fragile balance between control and possibility—and what it truly means to choose.

Back Cover

What if time was never meant to be fixed?

A solitary traveler arrives in Paris. At first, the city feels familiar—quiet streets, warm light, and the steady rhythm of life unfolding. But something begins to shift. Moments repeat. Reflections move before she does. And just ahead, always out of reach, another version of herself appears.

Drawn into a hidden network beneath the city, she uncovers a system designed to do the impossible: stabilize time itself. But stability comes at a cost. One path. One outcome. No correction. No second chances.

As the system begins to collapse toward a single irreversible future, she is forced to confront a final decision: fix time forever, or keep it alive—and uncertain.

A novel of time, memory, and choice.

Also by Mark Anderson

- *Tommi the Green Tomato (Bilingual Series)*
- *The Alignment Echo (Books I, II, III) - SciFi*
- *The Accidental Genius & Snackcidents (Cookbook)*
- *Does AI Scare You? Yes. No. Maybe.*
- *Finnish with Purpose*
- *Swedish and Portuguese with Purpose - Coming Soon*

The Meridian Series

Where time is not fixed—and neither is choice.

Book 1: *The Meridian Paris Protocol*

The system is discovered.

A solitary traveler arrives in Paris and uncovers a hidden structure designed to stabilize time itself.
But stability demands a single outcome—and the cost of removing uncertainty may be everything.

Book 2: *The London Recurrence*

The system resists control.
Coming Soon

As intervention replaces observation, the system begins to react—repeating, correcting, and narrowing possibility.
Control becomes consequence, and precision reveals its limits.

Book 3: *The Tokyo Convergence*

The system becomes something else.

In Tokyo, the boundaries between observer and system collapse.
Multiple paths intersect, and a new form of time begins to emerge—one that cannot be contained, predicted, or undone.

www.ingramcontent.com/pod-product-compliance
Lightning Source LLC
LaVergne TN
LVHW010950110826
845149LV00015B/3288

* 9 7 9 8 9 9 5 8 0 8 5 0 3 *